The Memoirs

of

Beatrice Miller

by

Jeannie G Bruenning

Chapter One

Beatrice Miller fell somewhere in the middle of eight children. Of all the Miller children, Beatrice was organized, punctual, and a true sales person. She was willing to sell anything for a price. Her lunches were far more than she could ever eat; selling it ala cart gave her a nice little profit.

From the time she could walk, playing store was Beatrice's favorite game. She would collect items for around the house, set them up on display, and invite her siblings to shop. When she was a little older, Mother caught her sneaking out of the house with a small box. When asked what was in it, she simply replied, "Stuff." It wasn't until a few days later that Mother was informed by a neighbor; Beatrice was going door to door selling her goods. After that, Beatrice Miller was only allowed to set up shop in her bedroom, which she did daily.

The Miller's lived in Greenville, a small Midwest town that did not offer much in the way of shopping.

Greenville's Main Street was no more than two blocks long. The biggest shop in those two blocks was Uncle Walter's Mercantile. Reis Mercantile had been around as long as the town had. Beatrice's Grandfather had started it shortly after he and Grandma Myrtle came to town. Uncle Walter started working when he was a teenager and never left. When Grandpa Reis passed on, Uncle Walter was the obvious choice to take over. Beatrice loved the Mercantile; she went whenever Mother allowed her to.

Uncle Walter offered positions to all his nieces and nephews when they became of working age. Beatrice couldn't wait for her twelfth birthday. She had spent her lifetime managing the store she had created in her bedroom and after years in business, it was time to close her doors and move on. She was certain she would be ready for real customers, real merchandise, and real money.

Beatrice's older siblings had done their stint in the Mercantile, and although each was grateful for the opportunity, none of them wanted to make it their life. Beatrice could not understand such a choice. For her, there was no other place she wanted to be than in a store. As her twelfth birthday drew close, her anticipation grew.

Mother was known for her parties and Beatrice's twelfth birthday party did not disappoint. Aunt Ruth came on the train for the celebration. Aunt Ruth lived in the big city and Beatrice thought her life was most likely the most exciting one she could imagine. Ruth stayed all weekend assisting Mother with preparations and spending time with Uncle Walter whenever she could sneak away.

The night before her first day, Beatrice Miller finished dinner, said goodnight to Mother and Father, kissed the little ones and retired to her room. She placed her handmade Do Not Disturb sign on the door. She had much to do to prepare for the next day and could not be bothered. Beatrice laid out her new dress that Father bought her just for this very occasion. He had asked Aunt Ruth to pick out a dress she thought that Beatrice would like and bring it with her to the birthday party. When Beatrice opened it, she couldn't believe how beautiful it was. She knew immediately that it would be what she wore on her first day of work. Beatrice shined her Sunday church shoes and set them next to her bed. She brushed her hair and pulled it up into a pony tail. Beatrice changed into her night gown, got under the covers, and laid there for hours waiting for the sun to rise.

The next morning, as Mother entered the kitchen to start the day, she found Beatrice dressed and sitting at the window. "Beatrice, how long have you been down here?"

"A little while, Father said he needed to do something in the barn before breakfast, but he'll be back," she said.

"You were up before Father?"

"Yes," she said with confidence.

"Bea, you're going to be very tired today. You need to get your sleep."

"I just couldn't Mother. I'll make up for it tonight."

Mother began making breakfast as each of the children made their way downstairs. Father returned with a jug of fresh milk and a basket of eggs. The kitchen came alive, but Beatrice did not notice. Her eyes were set on the clock, watching each minute tick by.

At the appropriate time, Beatrice put on her coat, picked up the lunch Mother prepared for her. She gave Mother a kiss and as she turned to do the same to Father, realized he was standing by the door with keys in his hand.

"On your first day, you will be escorted to work," Father said with a grin.

"Really?" Beatrice said. She had never known Father to offer to escort anyone anywhere. He believed that if you were old enough to have somewhere to go, you were certainly old enough to figure out how to get there.

Beatrice followed Father to the truck with a chorus of young voices wishing her well on her first day. The short drive was done in silence for Beatrice's anticipation stole any conversation from her. As Father pulled in front of the Mercantile, he said, "You're early, Uncle Walter will appreciate that."

"Yes, sir," Beatrice said with a smile and nod. She grabbed the door handle, looked back at Father who sent her off with a wink and she opened the door.

She had planned to be ten minutes early, but with Father offering to drive her, she was even earlier. She had overheard Uncle Walter confess that he would not tolerate tardiness and that was why Cousin Fred was let go. She would not be like Cousin Fred. She wasn't sure what *let go* meant, but it would never be a term used in conjunction with her name. If there was any *letting go* to do, she would be the one - letting go. Beatrice waited on the front porch until the appropriate time. Ten minutes, not one earlier or later.

Uncle Walter welcomed her with a handshake as, according to him, hugging was not proper in the business world. Proper employees greeted each other with a strong, bold handshake. It was the professional way of doing things. Beatrice had been practicing her handshake for some time now. There were many of the boys at school that stayed clear of her in recent days as their hands could take no more of Beatrice's professional greeting.

Uncle Walter showed her to the back hall where she had her very own hook to hang her coat and shelf for any personal belongings. Beatrice placed her lunch on the shelf. As far as hooks and shelves went, these were acceptable. Beatrice decided right then that when she had a shop of her own, her hooks and shelves would have far more personality.

On her first day, Beatrice Miller was assigned to the fabric bins. Beatrice's mother was an accomplished seamstress and Uncle Walter thought that starting with something familiar would make Beatrice's first day much more enjoyable. Beatrice took the assignment with her usual smile and nod. Truth be told, she hated fabric. She had held, measured, and folded so much fabric in her life that she would like to never see another bolt. Beatrice had seen pictures of dresses that did not require mothers to sew. They were already made; those were the dresses she wanted to sell. Not stuffy old fabric that had to be turned into something. She wanted the finished product.

Beatrice kept busy all day. She folded, dusted, reorganized, talked to customers, and swept the floor. Uncle Walter watched in delight, Beatrice was a natural. As the last customer left the store, Uncle Walter asked Beatrice to lock the door behind them. As Beatrice turned the knob, she knew she was home. This is where she would spend the rest of her life. She would work hard, and someday she would be the shop keeper.

Uncle Walter accompanied her to the back hall where she collected her coat from the hook and her belongings from the shelf. As she turned, Uncle Walter held out his hand and Beatrice shook it.

"Quite a grip you have there," Uncle Walter said.

"Yes sir, I've been practicing," Beatrice replied.

"Good day today, my dear. A good day indeed. Will you be back tomorrow?" he asked.

"Yes sir," Beatrice said confidently. "Tomorrow - and every day after that."

"Good!" said Uncle Walter. "Just a few more days working with fabric and then on to dry goods." Beatrice loosed her grip. "Something wrong?" he asked.

"No sir, I look forward to it," she said quite convincingly.

They walked to the front door and as Uncle Walter unlatched the lock, Beatrice sighed. *A few more days with those awful bolts of fabrics,* she thought. As she passed through the door and heard the lock latch once again, she turned, smiled and waved causing her to trip on the first step off the porch. Beatrice caught herself and continued on. With each step she noticed the ache that began running up her shins, it seemed to be traveling up from her feet. *These damn shoes,* she thought. Beatrice Miller had never used that word before. She had only ever heard one person say that word. Father used it frequently when he was angry or frustrated. It sounded bold when Father said it. It sounded bold when Beatrice said it, even if she hadn't spoken it out loud. It felt like a useful word. *I don't care what Mother says, I'm wearing my boots tomorrow. This will be the last day my feet will hurt.*

As the days and weeks passed, Beatrice Miller showed up to work ten minutes early, stylishly dressed from head to ankle. She learned about dry goods, hardware, and every other product Uncle Walter sold. On her sixth month anniversary, Uncle Walter greeted her energetically at the door.

"Good morning, my dear!" he said as he held out his hand. Beatrice grasped it and shook it firmly. "Still a great grip you have there." Beatrice smiled. "Today, you are graduating to the cash register."

Beatrice began shaking Uncle Walter's hand vigorously. "Oh, thank you! Thank you!" she said.

Beatrice walked to the back hall, hung her coat on the hook and placed her belongings on the shelf. As she turned, Uncle Walter held out his hand, in it was a shiny gold pin.

"This is for you," he said. "It is to commemorate your accomplishments on the selling floor and shows that you are now ready to move up in the world." Beatrice raised her head in honor as Uncle Walter pinned it to her collar.

"I will wear it always," she said. Uncle Walter stretched out his arms as if he was expecting a hug, but Beatrice would have nothing of it. She confidently held out her hand. Uncle Walter hesitated for just a moment, then laughed and shook her hand joyously.

"Are you ready to get started?" he asked.

"Yes sir," she replied.

The two walked over to the register. Beatrice thought it to be the most beautiful thing she had ever seen. She had heard stories of pirates and treasure chests and could not imagine that any treasure ever found could be more beautiful as Uncle Walter's cash register.

She had admired it, well, forever; ever since she could remember visiting Uncle Walter's store with her mother. Its brass finished looked like gold to Beatrice and no one could convince her otherwise. She loved the picture of the hand that pointed to two numbers; one being the clerk number and the other the sale price. She would have a clerk number someday; she just knew it.

Uncle Walter assigned her number 8 as her very own. He showed her how to enter her number 8 by pushing the yellow buttons. The red buttons was dollars, the next row was ten cents, and the last row was ones. One, tens and hundreds, she had learned that in first-grade. Now she was all grown up, had a job complete with a clerk number, and she remembered her ones, tens, and hundreds.

After entering the sale price, Uncle Walter grabbed hold of the lever handle that stuck out on the right side and pulled it down. It made a sound that gave Beatrice goose bumps. It was a sort of a ring, she could only imagine was the sound that angels make when children are good, or at least that is what Grandma Reis used to tell her.

Beatrice watched as the number 8 and 1.35 showed up at the top. She was convinced that Uncle Walter was the most brilliant man she had, or would, ever meet. To think that he has things in his store that people need, and even some things they just want, and they pay him money for it just so he can go out and buy more things so more people can come in an pay him more money. Brilliant may not have been the right word, he was beyond brilliant, but Beatrice Miller couldn't think of a word to describe that, her vocabulary was far too limited.

"Now it is your turn," instructed Uncle Walter. "Pretend I am a customer and I want to purchase these gloves." Uncle Walter reached across the counter and selected a pair of gloves from the display. The sign above them read; SALE $.75.

Beatrice thoughtfully and accurately pressed the yellow number 8, the 70 and the 5. She then grabbed the handle on the side lever with her right hand. With great precision she pulled the lever down and heard the sound of angels.

"Very nicely done," said Uncle Walter. "Here is my dollar."

Uncle Walter handed her a pretend dollar bill. Beatrice smiled, took the bill, said, "Thank you." She then pressed the large rectangular button in the center of the register.

"You've been observing. I didn't show you how to do that," Uncle Walter said.

"Yes sir, ever since I can remember," she said with great excitement.

The wooden drawer popped open and Beatrice's mouth dropped. She had never seen so much money. The drawer was divided into little sections; each section containing one type of coin or bill. She had finally seen the pot of gold. She had found her pirates treasure. Uncle Walter was not only the most brilliant man she had ever known, he must be the richest!

Beatrice traced the letters - N a t i o n a l - that were fixed to the front of the cash drawer. *National*, even its name sounded regal. Beatrice remembered when she was just a child of three or four, standing on the other side of the counter, gazing up at this amazing gold cash register, hoping that some day she would make the angel bell ring. Beatrice made the angel bell ring all day long.

Today she was all grown, and at the age of twelve and a half, and with Uncle Walter's expert training, she had a clerk number and was allowed to ring customers transactions, take their money and make the angel bell ring all on her own. She knew this is what she wanted to do for the rest of her life.

Chapter Two

Alma Breckschnieder lived a privileged life. Her mother didn't sew, she didn't need to. Alma's dresses were bought already assembled at the department store. Alma and Beatrice had two things in common; the first was that they were the same age. Beatrice had worked weekends with Uncle Walter until she was finished with school. With Mother and Father's blessing and Uncle Walter's great delight, Beatrice decided to make Reis Mercantile her career at the age of fourteen. The other common thread that connected these two girls was that both their uncles owned stores. Beatrice's Uncle Walter had his mercantile and Alma's Uncle Fredrick owned the five story department store in the heart of the big city.

Breckschnieder's was the largest and most modern store in five states. One of Uncle Walter's venders had been there and on his next delivery to the Mercantile, provided Uncle Walter with all the details.

" There's five stories," he began.

"Five stories? How does he fill it?" Uncle Walter interrupted.

"He fills it just fine. Makes trips across the ocean several times a year. He has a whole team of people whose only job is to find product."

"A whole team, you say?"

"And that's not all. He has a team of people designing and making things that are exclusively for Breckschnieder."

"Does he have factories?"

"Yea, I guess. With five stories to fill, I reckon one story could be a factory."

"How much of it have you seen?"

"Deliveries are made around the back of the store. Took us an hour just to find the entrance."

Uncle Walter laughed, "A whole hour you say?"

"There is nothing else on the entire city block. The whole block is Breckschnieder's."

"No."

"Yes. The entrance is an ally on the back side."

"Did they let you look around?"

"No. Had to change clothes and enter around the front. There are also five entrances."

"Five?"

"God's truth. Five entrances and between them are giant windows for display. One was big enough to set up an entire room of a house. They could get a car in there and I bet someday he'll try it." The purveyor looked around the Mercantile, "It would take your entire inventory to fill his windows." Both men laughed at the thought. Beatrice stood behind the counter listening to every word.

"I can't imagine," Uncle Walter said.

"Did I tell you about the restaurants?" Uncle Walter shook his head. "There are five of those as well. Anything you want to eat, they have it. One restaurant is just for women and each one was dressed more elegantly then the next."

"If it was for women only, how did you get in?"

"You can look in, just can't enter. It was like a painting; dark maple lined the walls, chandeliers hanging from the ceiling – all eclectic too."

"No!"

"Yes! I told you it's amazing. Don't know how many people work there but there's a lot." The purveyor paused for a moment. "His workers live there. Well, some of them do."

"Live there? You mean like close by?"

"Just across the street. Breckschnieder bought one of the apartment buildings and lets any of his clerks who don't have a place in the city to live there. They get a small apartment and there's a huge dining room on the first floor; he even provides them with clothes to wear. They all look the same, guess that's how he keeps control."

"They don't have family?"

"They got family. When they're hired, they move in; a bed, meals, uniform, not a bad deal if you ask me." He looked at Beatrice who was lost in imagining her apartment. "You should take a trip," the purveyor suggested. "I'll hook you up with our deliveries and you can see the inside and out." Uncle Walter rubbed his forehead and slowly shook his head.

"I'll go with you, Uncle," Beatrice said so caught up their conversation that she could envision every detail.

"That's a swell idea! Walt, you should take her along."

"We'll see, we'll see," Uncle Walter said.

For the next month Beatrice took every opportunity to remind Walter of the offer to see Breckschnieder's.

Between Beatrice's constant urging and his own curiosity, Uncle Walter and Beatrice Miller journeyed to the big city to see Breckschnieder's first hand.

Beatrice's mother insisted that they travel by train. She had arranged for her sister to meet them at the station and take them home for a good meal. They could spend the afternoon at Breckschnieder's, but she insisted they be back at Aunt Ruth's by dinner time and back on the train the next morning. The two agreed. However, Beatrice was sure she could convince Aunt Ruth to let them eat at least one meal at Breckschnieder's. This may be her only chance and she wanted to experience all of it.

The night before their expedition, sleep did not visit Beatrice. It tried, even knocked on the door a few times, but she would have nothing of it. Her room so full of excitement, anticipation, and expectations, that even if sleep had found its way in, it would have been trampled in her dreams.

At the light of day, Mother found Beatrice dressed, packed and sitting next to the fire in the kitchen. "Let me make you some breakfast," Mother said.

"I'm far too excited to eat," she said. "When is Uncle going to be here?"

"Beatrice, you must have something to eat before you go, take your coat off and sit at the table."

Beatrice reluctantly removed her coat and took her seat as Mother toasted the bread and set it on the table with a bowl of fresh strawberries. "How about a cup of cocoa?" she asked. Beatrice nodded. "I've pack you a little snack for the train and Aunt Ruth will meet you at the station. She's promised me that she will take you home for lunch before sending you out. Beatrice," her mother said looking directly at her. Beatrice knew she was getting ready to hear what Mother felt was the most important instruction yet. "Don't leave Uncle's side. Not even for a moment." Mother waited for her acknowledgment. Beatrice nodded. "I don't know how you talked me into this? I should not have agreed. You're much too young to be making such a trip without me."

"I'm fifteen and a half. I'll be fine. I'll keep Uncle in my sight at all times."

"Thank you. And when you are at Aunt..."

"When I am at Aunt Ruth's, I'll remember my manners; I won't expect her to wait on me. I'll make my bed in the morning and I'll remember to thank her when we leave."

"Thank you," Mother said once again. She smiled. Beatrice was growing up. She had proven to be a hard worker and Walter had nothing but praise for her. Out of all her children, Beatrice was not one she needed to worry about.

The other children began finding their way to the kitchen as Beatrice heard Uncle Walter's truck come up the drive. She sprang to her feet, grabbed her coat and satchel. Mother handed her the small package of snacks she had prepared. Beatrice leaned over and kissed her cheek, "Don't worry, we'll be fine." Mother nodded. Beatrice was out the door and in the truck in a flash.

It was a short ride to the station. Beatrice had taken the train many times to visit Aunt Ruth, but each of those times she had her younger brothers and sisters in tow. Today she had no one else to think about, no one to keep up with, no one to hold hands with. Today, she was Beatrice Miller traveler.

"Do you have our tickets?" Uncle Walter asked.

Fear and worry quickly replaced Beatrice's excitement. "No Uncle, you have them."

Uncle Walter patted his coat pocket. Beatrice stood frozen in her concern. "Ah, yes. There they are." Beatrice found her breath once again. "Right there where I put them," he said with a mischievous grin.

 The two adventurers boarded the train and sat in the middle compartment. Uncle Walter graciously offered Beatrice the window seat in which she took without hesitation. The whistle blew, the conductor shouted, "All aboard." And they were off.

"What's you got in there?"

"Mother made us snacks," Beatrice said as she handed over the package.

"Don't you want any?"

"No, couldn't eat. Mother already forced me to eat breakfast – couldn't take another bite."

As the train rolled along the tracks, Beatrice took in the country side. She loved the country, but it wasn't where she wanted to live. *The country is for visiting,* she thought. *I'm a city girl.* Farm after farm pass by and then suddenly there were buildings. Large warehouses at first, then large homes, a school yard, a church, and a bank. The closer they got to the city, the closer the building sat. The buildings passed by her window at such a rate that she felt the train must be picking up speed. In the distance she could see a tall building that had not been there before. Beatrice tried counting the floors, twelve is what she thought.

"They're getting taller and taller," Uncle Walter said. Beatrice had almost forgotten he was sitting next to her.

"It's got at least twelve floors," she said.

"They are planning a twenty story building."

"Can you imagine what it would be like to work on the top floor of a twenty story building?"

"Not something I ever plan on doing," Uncle said.

"I do," Beatrice said. "I will love to live on the top floor."

Beatrice felt the train slowing and her excitement growing. The brakes squealed, the whistle blew, and billows of steam escaped as the train came to a complete stop and jerked back a bit. Uncle Walter took the lead and Beatrice stayed close behind.

As they entered the station, Beatrice spotted Aunt Ruth waving her hands wildly in the air. She waved back, grabbed Uncle's arm and directed him to her.

Aunt Ruth stretched on her tip toes to greet Walter with a kiss, "Looking good Brother," she said and then captured Beatrice in her arms. "My darling, you made it! So glad you are here! We are going to have so much fun today – an adventure is waiting." She reached out and took Beatrice's satchel, "Is this all you brought? We'll have to find you a much larger one to take back with you. I may have one - oh," Ruth waved her hand in front of her as if to wipe her words away, "we'll just buy you one of your own. I'm sure you'll make use of it."

Aunt Ruth hooked arms with Walter and keeping her other arm wrapped around Beatrice's shoulders, began to walk to the exit.

"You're house first?" Walter asked.

"Of course not! Beatrice doesn't want to eat cold sandwiches at my house. She's here for an adventure, aren't you my dear? If you want to see Breckschnieder's then we need to go there directly. I'm thinking lunch and dinner. Sound good to you Bea?" Beatrice smiled. "That's what I thought."

Beatrice felt a sudden knot forming in her stomach. It wasn't like her to go against Mother's wishes. She didn't see any danger in the sudden change of plans. After all, she was in Aunt Ruth and Uncle Walter's care, if they felt is was appropriate, than who was she to speak up against them.

As they exited the building Walter hesitated. "No taxi today," Ruth instructed. "We're walking. It's just about six blocks. You need the exercise." Walter laughed and Beatrice looked up to take in the cityscape.

The sidewalk was filled with people. *People going places, doing things,* Beatrice thought. Beatrice imagined she was one of those people. She would have a small apartment just a few blocks from where she worked. She would live in the city; it's where she was meant to live. She knew it.

"And there it..." Aunt Ruth said as they turned the corner. "There it is!"

"Holy..." Uncle Walter began.

"Watch it!" interrupted Ruth. "What do you think, dear?"

Beatrice couldn't think, there wasn't any room in her brain for thinking. It was far too busy experiencing. Standing in front of her was a five story building made of the whitest stone she had ever seen. And Uncle Walter's delivery man was right; the windows were large enough to put a car into. Giant flags waved just above the entrance. On the corner of the building were huge clocks telling her she needed to hurry.

The three walked around the exterior looking at each window display; each more gorgeous than the last, each telling a story. There were life size figures in the windows displaying coats, dresses, shoes and even nightgowns. Beatrice was spellbound as she stood looking into the last window which displayed six models wearing evening gowns and draped in jewelry, and fur coats. The floor had been filled with blue tissue paper and gold streamers hung from the ceiling. Beatrice saw her reflection in the window. She didn't want to be a model, she wanted to be the one who dressed the models, to place them in the windows, and decide what color tissue would be used. For one brief moment, Beatrice Miller saw herself in the world she knew she was born to live.

"Anyone ready to eat?" Aunt Ruth asked.

Chapter Three

Aunt Ruth took Beatrice's arm and headed for the front entrance. Uncle Walter stayed close behind. There was a man in uniform standing on the outside of the doors. It was his job to greet customers as he opened the door for them.

"Good morning, Ruth," he said as he reached for the door. "Are these our expected guests?"

"Yes, Bernard, they are. Arrived safe and sound," Aunt Ruth replied.

"You are having lunch on the fourth floor," said Bernard.

"Thank you Bernard," Aunt Ruth said.

Bernard looked directly at Beatrice, "Enjoy your special day," he said. Beatrice smiled. As Uncle Walter passed, Bernard saluted and said, "Good day Sir." Beatrice noticed that Uncle Walter straightened up a bit as he nodded in acknowledgement.

Beatrice pulled Aunt Ruth close to her, "he knows your name," she whispered. Aunt Ruth winked and kept walking.

Beatrice tried keeping up with Aunt Ruth but there was just so much to see. Aisles of counters, displayed with scarves, gloves, jewelry, and perfumes. The ladies behind the counter were all dressed in black taffeta dresses. Their hair was pulled up with ringlets cascading along their faces. Beatrice couldn't find one that wasn't engaged in conversation with a customer.

At every counter was a cash register. Not like the National that she and Uncle Walter used. These were silver, not brass, which made them shine even more. They were smaller and didn't have the big wooded cash drawer at the bottom. The trio passed by as a clerk was finishing a sale. Beatrice waited for it. And then she heard it, the angel bell, it made her giggle. Aunt Ruth glanced over to see what was so entertaining. Beatrice squeezed her arm and shrugged her shoulders. Her excitement was uncontainable.

As they approached the atrium in the center of the store, Beatrice let go of Aunt Ruth's arm. This was beauty as she had never seen. In the center of the atrium was a water fountain, shooting water at least two stories high. The bottom of it was lined with coins. She had heard of throwing coins into a fountain for good luck, or to make wishes come true, but she had never actually seen it. There were hundreds of coins twinkling at the bottom of the shallow pool and Beatrice's dreams were coming true.

As Beatrice looked up, she gasped. The ceiling was two, three, four, five stories above her. Each floor between had open railings allowing for guests to look down on the fountain. As she looked up, she reached back and took Uncle Walter's hand. He too was mesmerized by the size and beauty of the atrium.

"Uncle, have you ever?" Beatrice said.

"Never, my dear. Never in my entire life..."

"On the second floor," Aunt Ruth began as she pointed up, "you will find the woman's department. Anything and everything you would ever want to wear. The finest dresses, furs, and even negligees." Aunt Ruth grinned and raised her eyebrows. Beatrice blushed. "On the third floor is children's clothing and toys. There is a train set up there that I could stand and watch for hours. The fourth floor is furniture. They have little rooms all set up as if it's a room in your home. We'll walk through the tableware department. There are so many patterns that if you bought one of each, you could eat for three months on a different plate." Beatrice laughed at the idea.

"The fifth floor is almost all restaurants and offices. That is where Fredrick works. Now, as Bernard said, we have an appointment on the fourth floor. Shall we?" Aunt Ruth asked.

Uncle Walter and Beatrice nodded as Aunt Ruth began to walk toward the elevators. As the elevator doors opened, Beatrice had to step aside to allow those exiting to pass.

"Good day, Ruth," said the elevator operator.

"Hello, Janice. How is your day going?"

"Just fine. I take it these are our special guests?"

"Yes, arrived safe and sound this morning."

"Been here long?"

"No, just long enough to look at the windows and take a spin around the atrium. But we have reservations."

"Yes, you do. Come on in. I'll get you to four in a flash."

Aunt Ruth stepped into the elevator and gently pulled Beatrice with her. Uncle Walter hesitated for just a second, then forced his right leg to take a step in.

"All the way in please, don't want you to get stuck in the door," the attendant said.

The doors closed and Beatrice Miller was taking her first trip in a real elevator. She watched as the numbers above the door lit up. One, two, three, four; the elevator came to a stop and the attendant pushed the doors open.

"Enjoy," she said as the three exited.

"Thank you," Beatrice said.

Aunt Ruth was right, the fourth floor was a collection of little rooms all set up as if they were room in your home. There were living rooms, dining rooms, bedrooms. Beatrice wanted to stop at each and sit on the sofas, try a chair or two, or just feel the texture of the fabrics. But Aunt Ruth walked as if they were on a mission.

As they drew closer to where they would be served lunch, Beatrice couldn't help but notice the increase of noise; voices in conversation, plates being stacked and orders being taken. Aunt Ruth headed to a podium at the entrance.

"Ruth, so glad to see you. We've been waiting. Welcome Mr. Ries," the attendant reached out his hand in greeting. "And this must be Beatrice. Ruth, you are right. I see the resemblance. You are delightful. Your table is ready, follow me." Aunt Ruth, Beatrice Miller and Uncle Walter followed the attendant to a corner table which looked out over the city. "A table with the best view in the building." He held the chair for Aunt Ruth. Uncle Walter and Beatrice took their own seats. "And here are your menus. It is just so good to finally meet you. Ruth has told us so much about you. It's as if you are already family."

"You can order whatever you want. Today is my treat." Aunt Ruth leaned over and pointed to the roast beef platter, "Walt, you should try that, you'll love it. And Bea, I would recommend the chicken-pot-pie, it's heavenly. There is also the Breckschnieder sandwich, tough choice. I love them all."

Uncle Walter and Beatrice looked over the menu briefly before folding them and setting them down. Beatrice leaned toward Ruth, "How do you know everyone?" Beatrice asked.

Aunt Ruth laughed, "It must seem like I live here. I am here a lot; it's a wonderful place to spend time. Fredrick, or I should say, Mr. Breckschnieder's wife was one of my dearest friends. Walt, you remember Doris Blume?"

"Doris, you two were inseparable as kids."

"My very, very best friend in the entire world. Doris's family moved to the city when we were teens. She and Fredrick met at a small shop where she was working as a clerk. They were married just about the time William and I were. We stayed in touch, and when I moved here with William, Doris and I connected as if no time had passed."

"Then Doris became ill and it was quite serious. She was in and out of the hospital for a few years before the doctors said there was nothing they could do for her. William and I spent every free moment we had with Fredrick and Doris during that time. When

Doris passed, we made sure we stayed in touch with Fredrick. It was just before he opened this place, and he needed a lot of support. Doris never had a chance to see Breckschnieder's. It still breaks my heart to think of it." Aunt Ruth took a sip of water.

Uncle Walter cleared his voice, "Ruth, I never put it together that Doris had married The Breckschnieder."

"You may have never heard her last name, she just always been Doris," Ruth replied.

"I had no idea," Walt said.

"When my beloved William died, Fredrick and I remained close friends. Neither of us have children. William left me well cared for, and this store is Fredrick's first born. I feel in a way, that I am helping him raise his only child. He is a dear man and I cherish our friendship. You'll meet him at dinner. He's promised to join us."

"He's joining us for dinner?" Uncle Walter asked.

"Yes, is there a problem?"

Walter coughed and cleared his throat again. "No," Uncle Walter said very slowly. "I just wasn't expecting to meet the top man."

"How wonderful!" Beatrice exclaimed and grabbed Uncle Walter's arm with both hands. "How often do you get to meet someone who is just like you?"

"Well, not just like," Walter responded.

"Sure he is! You both own your very own shops!" Beatrice said.

"I suppose. But we really aren't the same. I appreciate the fact that you think so," Uncle Walter said as he gave Beatrice a hug.

"You are more alike than you want to admit," Aunt Ruth said. "You and Fredrick are two of my favorite men and that has to count for something."

"If you say so," Walter said.

"Are we ready to order?" A server was now standing at the end of the table.

Aunt Ruth was right, Uncle Walter loved his roast beef and Beatrice didn't want her chicken-pot-pie to end even though she couldn't find room for another bite. Aunt Ruth ate every bit of her Breckschnieder Sandwich but not without first forcing her guest to try it.

After lunch, the trio headed out once again to explore five stories of merchandise. Aunt Ruth made sure they took time to sit down to rest. Uncle Walter was over whelmed thinking of what it must take to run such an operation and Beatrice couldn't stop thinking how much fun it must be to work there.

"We have 6:30 p.m. reservations on the fifth floor," Aunt Ruth informed her guests. "We'll be eating at Fredrick's favorite restaurant."

At 6:25 p.m. the three entered the fifth floor express elevator. As they exited, they found themselves in a large lobby leading to three separate entrances. As they passed the first, Aunt Ruth stopped, "This is the dining room for women only." The room was paneled with dark maple wood. A chrisom carpet covered the floor and chrisom floral fabric covered the chair cushions. There were candles and beautiful flower arrangements on each table.

"Why is there no one in there?" Beatrice asked.

"Because, they are all at home," Aunt Ruth replied. "They only serve from 10:00 a.m. to 3:00 p.m. as that is the appropriate time for married women to head home to their own families." From the next entrance Beatrice could hear music. "This is the dining room." Gold leaf glimmered at the top of the walls. Real candelabras illuminated the table. A piano sat in the center of the room. This evening there was a string quartet that played though the evening.

"Is this were we are eating?" Beatrice asked.

"Not tonight, dear." Aunt Ruth pointed to the last door, "That's Fredrick's favorite. I let him choose tonight. Shall we? I'm sure he is already seated."

Aunt Ruth led the way and as Uncle Walter turned the corner, he let out a burst of laughter. The room looked exactly like the dining car on the train. Every detail was captured. The table and seats, the windows were the size of the windows on a train. The waiters were dressed in conductor uniforms. A long steal bar separated the dining area from the kitchen allowing for the guest to watch their food being prepared. The chefs were clad in uniforms resembling train engineers'. From the far corner of the room they heard, "Ruth, over here."

Fredrick Breckschnieder was a tall, slim man, slightly younger than Uncle Walter. He had light blond hair and dark brown eyes. He stood and greeted Ruth with a gentle kiss on the cheek. Reaching out to shake Uncle Walter's hand, he said, "So honored to meet you, Walter. Ruth has told me so much about you. We are very similar, you and I, and I'm so pleased that you were able to find the time to visit. I trust someday soon, I'll reciprocate."

Uncle Walter shook hands. "A pleasure to meet you, as well. You have quite the operation here. I'm not sure reciprocating the visit would be worth your time."

"Nonsense," Fredrick said. "We are the same you and I. There is very little difference in what we do, except your task is much more difficult than mine. I have the greatest respect for what you do."

"Thank you," Uncle Walter said. He wasn't sure what else to say.

"And you must be Beatrice Miller?" Fredrick leaned over and offered his hand. Beatrice grabbed it. "Quite a handshake you have there. Tells a lot about a person. 'Never trust a weak handshake,' I always say."

"Uncle Walter says the same thing," Beatrice said wide eyed and grinning ear to ear.

"Wise man, he is," Fredrick said. "Are you ready to eat? The chefs are making my favorite."

The four took their seats. Beatrice and Uncle Walter sat on one side, with Beatrice seated next to the window. Fredrick and Aunt Ruth sat across from them. That night they feasted on giant sausages smothered in onions and resting in a fresh bun, the size that Beatrice had never seen. They tried something called an onion ring, which everyone loved. Beatrice could not figure out how such a thing could be made. Fredrick requested that Beatrice be allowed behind the steal counter and shown firsthand how to make a delicious ring. To drink, they were served Root-beer Floats. Uncle Walter got a tour of the kitchen, after he commented that he would love to serve such beverages at the Mercantile. Fredrick suggested he put in a soda fountain and even offered to help set it up.

It was a great night and the perfect ending to a wonder filled day. As Beatrice finished the last of her Root beer, she accidently made a loud slurping sound with her straw, Mr. Breckschnieder cleared his voice. Beatrice was suddenly nervous thinking he may be getting ready to correct her.

"Beatrice, your Aunt Ruth speaks very highly of you. In fact, I do believe if she had been blessed with a daughter, she would have wanted one just like you." Aunt Ruth tilted her head and looked warmly at Beatrice. "I understand your Uncle offers a position to all his nieces and nephews." Beatrice nodded. "I do the same. In fact, Alma will be starting next month, I think you are the same age. Would you ever consider coming and working for me?"

Beatrice almost choked. She looked at Uncle Walter who looked almost as surprised as she.

"Walter, I know I would be taking a very talented worker from you, but from what Ruth has told me, I believe you are the kind of person I want to be working behind my counters." Fredrick paused to allow his idea to settle. He reached in his pocket and pulled out a small white business card. Handing it to Beatrice, he said, "Here is my card. You think about it. Talk it over with your parents and, of course, Uncle Walter. If it is something you would like to explore, give me a call and we can schedule a trip for you and your mother to visit. I'm sure she will want to see where you would be living and I would like to meet her as well."

Beatrice took the card. *Fredrick Breckschnieder* was printed in bold letters on the front. Beatrice would have to use Uncle Walter's telephone as Father didn't think telephones were a necessity. Mother wouldn't let her leave. It would take all of Aunt Ruth's persistence to even get her to consider it. How could she leave Uncle Walter? Even though he was the most brilliant man she had ever met, could he make it without her? Could she make it without him?

Uncle Walter looked at Ruth and forced himself to smile. He put his arm around Beatrice's chair and gazed down at her. This was an opportunity of a life time and he knew it. He was pleased for her but it didn't make it any easier. Through his gentle smile, his heart was breaking.

Chapter Four

Aunt Ruth bought a ticket and accompanied Uncle Walter and Beatrice back to Greenville. She knew it was going to take some work to convince Beatrice's mother. She knew Walt was excited for her but was quite sure he wasn't going to be doing any convincing. If Bea was going to take this opportunity she would need some added support, and Ruth was just the person for the job.

Mother was so relieved to see Beatrice get out of the truck she didn't notice Ruth was sitting in the middle. As Ruth scooted across the seat and stepped out of the truck, she said, "Thought I'd give my old sis a visit."

"Ruth!" Mother exclaimed, "What are you doing here? It's been a while since you made a trip home."

"Thought it was time," she replied. "Had such a great time with this one that I just couldn't say goodbye so quickly. In fact, I think I want to keep her. She would love living in the city..."

"Over my dead body," Mother replied. "She's fine just where she is."

Beatrice smiled and gave Aunt Ruth a quick wink. She loved listening to her mother and aunt banter. She didn't get a chance to hear it often, but when it happened, she just wanted to pour a cup of cocoa, sit by the fire and enjoy the show.

And a show it was. For four days, Mother and Ruth debated Beatrice's future. Mother started with her age argument, which Ruth quickly defused by asking if she intended for Bea to stick around till she was thirty. "She will be sixteen next month. This is a chance of a lifetime. You were getting married at sixteen." An argument to which Mother had no response. She was married just before her seventeenth birthday and loved every day since.

For the next round, Mother pulled out the "It's too dangerous for a young girl to live all alone in the big city."

"Hogwash," Ruth said. "First of all, she won't be alone and second, she won't even have to worry about eating. It's all provided for her."

On the third day Mother dipped into her pity pocket. "I can't be that far away from her. What will I do?"

Ruth walked over to her and wrapped her arms around her, "You've had her for sixteen years, sis. Let me have her for a few before she's gone forever." Mother put her head on Ruth's shoulder and cried. Beatrice knew it was over, Mother had just surrendered.

That night at the dinner table the subject was not addressed until Father blurted out, "So when are you leaving?" There was a long pause as no one was quite sure how to respond. "She gave in, right? I figured it would take about three days, always does." Mother slapped Father on the arm, he caught her hand and squeezed it gently, brought it up to his lips and kissed it. "Fill me in on the details," he said.

Ruth looked at Beatrice and gave her the nod of approval. Beatrice told Father that she planned to go next month. Aunt Ruth would meet her at the station. She would spend a few nights at Aunt Ruth's before moving into her room. Father smiled and nodded in agreement.

"And what about Uncle Walter?" Father asked.

"Cousin Sophie just turned twelve and wants to give the Mercantile a try. Uncle Walter said I can train her!" Beatrice said.

"Sounds to me like it's all coming together. This is a great opportunity for you dear. Can't say I'm excited to see my little one go, but I wouldn't think of stopping you. You can do whatever you set your mind to, you get that from your mom. I have no doubt you'll be running the place by next year. That Mr. Breckschnieder doesn't know what he's in for."

"You may have a chance to tell him yourself," Ruth said. "Got a message from him this morning, he's planning to be here tomorrow afternoon."

"He's coming here?" Mother asked.

"That's what he said."

"Where will he stay? We can't have him here," she exclaimed.

"For heaven sakes, why not?" Father asked. Mother gave him her *don't be an idiot* look.

"He's not like that," Ruth said. "Fredrick is a rather simple man. Come to think of it, I don't think he has ever been here. Doris and I had planned a trip for the four of us to come back and show our beaus where we grew up, but that was just before Doris became ill. Fredrick has said several times that he still wanted to make the journey. Maybe you've given him a reason to, Bea."

The next day, Mother was up before Ruth busily cleaning the house and had already begun dinner by the time Ruth made it down stairs. Beatrice was dressed and washing a few stray dishes from the night before.

"He's not the Pope, sis," she said. She walked over and

poured herself a cup of coffee and then took a seat next to the fire. "You're going to love him, I just know you will." She took a sip of coffee. "You remember what a slob Doris was?" The thought of it made Ruth laugh, "Couldn't keep a clean house for anything. Fredrick loved her so – he's not going to see if there is dust under the chairs. He fed us sausages and onion rings for dinner, for Pete's sake. Relax. Why don't you come along with us?"

"Oh, I couldn't," Mother replied. "I'd be a nervous wreck. He may not see the dust but I will."

"Have it your way," Ruth said. "Bea, almost ready to go? I'll walk to the shop with you, let me finish this cup."

Ruth and Beatrice Miller walked arm in arm down the drive. They talked about all the things they were going to do in the city as soon as Beatrice arrived. At times, Beatrice thought, Aunt Ruth may be more excited than she was.

Ruth met Fredrick at the station. Fredrick was the last to get off the train. For a moment Ruth feared that he may have had a change of plans. When she finally saw him, she realized he was in no hurry. Fredrick greeted Ruth with an unexpected hug. "Ruth," he said, "Why haven't we ever come here before."

"Doris and I had planned a trip, but we never made it," Ruth said, taken a little back by Fredrick's unusual state of calm. Fredrick offered Ruth his arm and they walked across the platform toward the truck.

As Ruth pointed it out to Fredrick, she could see the excitement in him. Fredrick walked around the truck, leaving a figure mark in the dusty sides as he ran his finger along. He kicked the tires and chuckled. "It's got character," he said. "Would love to have a fleet of these!"

As Fredrick opened the door for Ruth he asked, "I suppose I can't drive it?"

"If you are a really good boy today, you can drive it back to the house," Ruth said settling in behind the wheel. Fredrick closed her door and went around to the passenger side.

They toured the little town of Greenville, stopping in front of the two story framed house where Doris grew up. "To think that my love lived in that house for more years than she did with me," Fredrick's eyes welled up slightly.

They drove passed the school where Doris and Ruth had become inseparable. They were the bestest of friends. "We got into a lot of trouble," Ruth said. "One of us was always coming up with hair brain ideas and the other planned them out. It's amazing we never killed anyone. Came close a few times, but with no success." Fredrick burst out laughing. "Seriously," Ruth said, "We really come close a few times."

They drove down Main Street which was only a few blocks long. "This is what it is all about," Fredrick said. "There are some days, I would give it all up to own one of these little shops. Know the first names of all my customers, and have a beer with them at the end of the night. I envy Walt. This is real life."

Ruth pulled the old truck into its appointed parking spot and the two got out. Fredrick walked around the front of the Mercantile. He removed his hat, rubbed the perspiration from his forehead and stood looking up at the sign that hung above the porch; Mercantile.

"What I wouldn't give," he said.

Beatrice walked out to greet the couple. "Welcome Mr. Breckschnieder," she said as she offered her hand in greeting.

Fredrick smiled as he took her hand, "Such a great grip you have there. I understand that you're going to be making a move soon."

"Yes, Sir!" Beatrice said with great excitement.

"I am so pleased," he said.

Uncle Walter emerged from the front door. He reached out his hand in greeting and Fredrick shook it boldly. "Excited to be here," he said. "You have quite the place here, Walt. Please show me around." And with that the two disappeared into the store.

Walter and Fredrick spent the remainder of the afternoon together; Fredrick asking him about his operation and Walter asking for his opinion. By the end of the day, they had planned where the new soda fountain should go, and what food Walter could start offering that would be easy to prepare yet allow for a good profit margin. They discussed the possibility of increasing the size of the store.

Fredrick suggested that Walter consider bringing in ready to wear clothing. Not a lot, but at least a small offering since it was the way of the future. He even offered that Walter come and talk with some of his buyers, they could recommend lines for him to start with, and suggest quantities as well. Uncle Walter found Fredrick to be all that Ruth had said. He hated to see Beatrice leave, but somehow it seemed not as painful knowing that she would be under his care.

"We need to get going," Ruth said attempting to bring an end to the afternoons visit. "Walter, will you be joining us for dinner?"

"Yes, I'll be there just after I lock up."

Ruth took Fredrick's arm and pulled him toward the truck. She handed him the keys and could feel the excitement in his anticipation. Fredrick opened the passenger door and assisted Ruth as she climbed into the truck. As he made his way around the truck, he noticed Beatrice stepping off the porch.

"Going our way?" he asked.

"Yes I am," she replied.

"May we offer you a lift?"

"Most certainly," Beatrice said with a giggle.

Bea ran around the truck and climbed in next to Aunt Ruth. Fredrick put the keys in the ignition, pumped the gas pedal a few times and turned the key. The old truck sputtered and chugged and finally turned over. "Love it!" Fredrick said. Ruth and Beatrice laughed at his excitement.

Mother had been working all day and set out a feast fit for a king. From the moment Father said "Amen" the discussion ignited and never lost fuel. It was almost ten o'clock before any of the adults, including Beatrice, left the table. That night Beatrice Miller transitioned from 'one of the kids' to adult.

The next morning, Mother was awakened by the smell of bacon frying, coffee brewing, and laughter. As she descended the stairs she could hear three men's voices. Father, Walter, and Fredrick were sitting around the table deep in discussion.

"Good morning, the Lady of the House," Fredrick offered.

"Who did all this?" Mother asked.

"Hope you don't mind," Fredrick offered. "It's been such a long time, couldn't help myself. What can I get for you? Here have a seat, let me serve you this morning."

Mother reluctantly took the seat next to Father. Fredrick took a china cup from the cupboard, "Hope you don't mind, I spotted these this morning and fell in love with them. I would use these every day if I were you."

"She keeps them for 'good'," Father offered. Mother nudged him with her elbow.

"Isn't it all good?" Fredrick replied. "Doris always said that life is all good. We can't wait for good to happen. We have to make it all good." Fredrick poured Mother a cup of coffee and placed it on the table in front of her. "There you are my lady. Now, what would be your fancy today?"

Mother picked up the cup and took a sip. "Surprise me," she said.

Fredrick Breckschnieder and Aunt Ruth boarded the train that morning after they said their farewells. They would be seeing Beatrice in ten days, just after her sixteenth birthday. Mother was no longer concerned for her safety, Father knew she would be successful, and Uncle Walter wanted to go with her.

Chapter Five

Beatrice's sixteenth birthday party turned into her going away party. Mother invited the entire town and everyone came. She woke early the next day, too excited to sleep, she had her things packed and was sitting in the kitchen when Mother came down the stairs.

"Bea, you're not leaving for hours," Mother said.

"Couldn't sleep," she said.

"Well, this gives us a little more time together. Everything packed?" Mother asked.

"I think so," she said.

The two women began preparing breakfast and their movements were like a choreographed dance. Each anticipating the other's next move, each finishing the other's task. Mother would miss this. As the rest of the family woke, the kitchen began to fill. No one was in a

hurry for the meal to be over. As the time ticked past, Beatrice kept a close eye on the clock.

"Father, I want to say good bye to Uncle Walter before I go," Beatrice said.

"I expected you would," he said. "We should be getting ready to go then, can't be late today."

Father carried Bea's trunk down the stairs and loaded it in the truck. As she said goodbye to all the younger Millers, each handed her a decoration to be hung in her new room. "It will make it feel like home," the youngest said. Beatrice took each one and tucked them safely in her satchel.

Mother was standing at the door as Beatrice took one last look around, making sure she hadn't missed anything. Mother took Bea's hands; she looked at her little girl who had somehow grown up overnight. "Be careful," Mother whispered, as she drew her close. "It's a big world out there; please promise me you'll be careful."

"I will," Beatrice said. She squeezed Mother one last time.

Father seemed to drive a little slower this morning. Beatrice kept looking at the speedometer; she had never known Father to take his time on the road. He pulled in front of the Mercantile and turned off the truck. They sat quietly for a few moments. "It was only a few years ago I drove you here for your first day."

"It was four years ago," Beatrice said.

"No, it couldn't be. Four years," Father replied. Beatrice reached out and grabbed hold of the door handle, she pulled on it slowly. As the door unlatched, she saw Uncle Walter step out on the porch. Beatrice flung the door open and ran with her arms wide open into his. They squeezed each other as tight as humanly possible.

"I'm going to miss you, my little one," Uncle Walter said as he kissed the top of her head.

"I'm going to miss you so much," Bea answered.

Sophie walked out onto the porch. Beatrice gave Walter one last squeeze and released him. Sophie handed her a small bouquet of flowers. "These are for you," she said. "They are to wish you well on your new job."

"Thank you Sophie," she said. "That was so thoughtful of you." She leaned over and gave Sophie a hug. "Take good care of him, if I hear anything less, I'll be on the next train back." Sophie laughed and took Uncle Walter's arm.

"I don't think I could ever replace you, but I'll do my best."

"You better get going, can't be late today," Walter said. Beatrice turned and stepped off the porch, she paused and spun back around and gave Walter one last hug. Father watched from the car and wiped a tear away.

The short drive to the train was a quiet one. Father was reliving the past sixteen years and Beatrice was imagining the next. They arrived just as the train did. Father loaded the trunk and Bea climbed aboard. She sat next to the window. As the engines began to roar, Father blew her a kiss and Beatrice caught it. She blew one back. Father caught it and held it next to his heart, and the train took off.

Beatrice watched as the country side passed her window, it was as beautiful as ever but she couldn't wait to begin seeing the warehouses. When the first came into view, she sighed, "We're almost there." As the train roared though the city, Beatrice realized that it looked different this time. It looked different because she was different. She was no longer a visitor, she was coming home.

As promised, Aunt Ruth met her at the station and had hired a taxi to take them back to her house. The driver loaded the trunk into the cab, opened the door for Ruth and Bea, and headed to the west side.

Uncle William had been a contractor; he built many of the commercial buildings in the city. In his career, he had only built one home, the one he offered to Ruth when they were married. It was a narrow brownstone style home with four stories. Each floor contained one or two rooms and a bathroom. On the first floor was a large kitchen and sitting area.

As Ruth unlocked the front door, they heard a chorus of barking dogs. Aunt Ruth never refused a dog that needed a home. As Ruth and Beatrice entered the house, they were greeted by six large hairy creatures, all very excited to see them. "I'll introduce you to Fred," Ruth said as she bent down to greet each one. "Fred arrived last week. We're not sure how he got separated from his owner. But we've not had any luck locating him. He's a big old bear, sweet as can be. Fred, say hello to Beatrice." On command, Fred barked. Beatrice bent down to say hello and was immediately engulfed by wet, slobbery kisses. "Boys, boys, back up," Ruth instructed. "Manners boys, remember your manners." The two laughed and shooed the six excited creatures away.

The cab driver pulled Beatrice's trunk up to the front door. Ruth tried to get him to take it to the third floor, but with no luck. The front door was as far as he was willing to go.

"You're taking the guest room on the third floor. Go get settled in, but you don't have too much time, I've got the rest of the day planned for us." For the next two days, Ruth and Beatrice were like school girls on a vacation. They ate at restaurants for every meal, they saw a show, visited the art museum; Ruth even arranged for Beatrice to be fitted for a new frock. "At sixteen one must begin to dress like a lady," Ruth said. "After all, you'll need something to wear when the first beau asks you out."

When the day finally arrived for Beatrice to report to Breckschnieder's, she woke with butterflies in her stomach. Aunt Ruth had prepared breakfast for her and a new dress was hanging on her bedroom door. Ruth pinned Beatrice's hair up and left a few ringlets to cascade down the side just like the ladies Beatrice had seen behind the counter. As she stood in front of the mirror, the butterflies disappeared. Reflected back was an image of a young woman, sophistically dressed and well put together. It was her job to exude the confidence that she felt at that moment. She could do this. She was ready to take on the new world that was about to reveal itself to her.

Beatrice reached out and retrieved the gold pin Uncle Walter had given her over four years ago. She carefully pinned it on her collar. "Now I'm ready."

After breakfast, Aunt Ruth hailed a taxi and she and Beatrice were off to Breckschnieder's. They arrived early. Ruth gave Beatrice a kiss on the cheek and whispered, "Show them what you're made of." Beatrice smiled, took a deep breath and forced her right foot to take the first step. Bernard greeted her at the door. He removed his cap and bowed as if she was royalty.

"You're first day?" he asked. "Welcome to Breckschnieder's." Beatrice nodded and entered the store.

As she walked though the isles, she listened closely, "I've got to hear it," she said softly. She was half way to the atrium before the first one sounded and then it was if they couldn't stop. At each register she passed, a customer was being rung up. The sound of the angel bells followed her through the store. She made her way to the atrium which seemed even more breathtaking then the first time she saw it. The elevator doors opened and she waited for it to empty. As she entered, she said, "Fifth floor, please."

"Yes, Ma'am," the attended replied. "You're first day?"

"Yes it is," Beatrice said with a smile.

"And right on time. Mr. Breckschnieder will appreciate that."

"Ten minutes early," Beatrice said. "Uncle Walter says is a clear indication of one's dedication to their job."

"Mr. Breckschnieder says the same thing!" the attendant said, as she closed the doors and pressed the five button. "You don't think they are the same person, do you?"

"They could be brothers," Beatrice replied with a laugh.

The elevator moved up slowly. Beatrice watched as the buttons lit up, two, three, four; a bell rang with they arrived at five. The attendant pushed the doors open, "Have a great first day, and welcome to Breckschnieder's!"

Beatrice walked down a long corridor looking for number 521. As she passed each door the numbers were going up. 519, 520, it must be the next one. 521 was just around the corner. Beatrice reached out and took hold of the knob. Tiny goose bumps began to make their way up her arm and across her shoulders.

As she opened the door, the woman behind the desk looked up. "Good morning," she said. "You must be Beatrice."

"Yes, Beatrice Miller."

"We are expecting you. I see you're a few minutes early. That's good, very good. Mr. Breckschnieder believes you can..."

"Tell ones dedication to the job by how early they arrive," Beatrice said with a smile.

"Exactly," the woman said. Surprised that Beatrice would have known Mr. Breckschnieder's words and curious as to how she would have known them.

"My Uncle Walter says the same thing," she offered.

The woman handed Beatrice a few forms and instructed her to take a seat and fill out the information carefully. "As soon as you are done with that, I'll take you to Mr. Breckschnieder's office. He wants to welcome you personally. Then you will be shown where to put your belongings, you did bring some things with you, correct?"

"Yes, Bernard said he would take care of them so I wouldn't have to haul them around."

"Good. That means that they will already be in your room. Lunch will be at 1:00 p.m., please try to keep a low profile while you're at lunch. This afternoon you are going to be our spy." Beatrice listened intently. "We want you to pretend you are a customer and see the store from the other side of the counter. Dinner is at 7:00 p.m. and there is a reception planned for our new arrivals. You aren't the only one starting today. Lights out at 10:00 p.m. and the breakfast bell will ring at 8:00 a.m. In the morning is your fitting followed by tour of the store. Martha will be taking you around. Pay attention, she knows every nook and cranny of this place. In the afternoon, I understand you will be starting in the fabric department."

Beatrice swallowed hard. "Something wrong?"

"No," Beatrice assured, "It's where I started my last position." Beatrice finished filling in the forms and handed them back.

"One more thing, today as you walk around the store, please take note of the dresses that sales girls are wearing. There are three styles. In the morning you will be expected to describe which style best fits you. Seems silly, I know, but I won't show up without that information if I were you." Beatrice nodded in agreement.

After looking over the paperwork briefly, she led Beatrice Miller to the end of the hall to where they were greeted by two large double doors. A guard stood at the entrance and as they approached, he nodded and opened the door for them. They walked passed a group of desks where four women sat answering phones and looking through stacks of files. Each raised their head and greeted the two as they passed by.

As they passed the last desk, a plump older woman looked out from behind a report she was reading. "Good morning," she said in a deep gruff voice. "He's waiting for you, go right in."

"Thank you," offered Beatrice's escort. Turning back she asked, "You ready?" Beatrice smiled. "I'm sure you are. You're a winner, could tell the second you stepped into my office." She reached down and opened the door. "Good morning, Mr. Breckschnieder, Beatrice Miller to see you."

Fredrick Breckschnieder leapt out of his chair and bolted around his long mahogany desk. It's was the biggest desk Beatrice had ever seen. It was longer than the table in her kitchen and that had enough room for twelve people to sit at. Mr. Breckschnieder reached out his hands expecting a hung, but Beatrice Miller would have nothing of it. She offered her hand and Mr. Breckschnieder took it.

"Welcome to Breckschnieder's. I'm so glad you are here. Have we gotten you settled in?"

"Her things are being delivered to her room as we speak. Bernard took care of it at the door."

"Well, if Bernard is on it, then there is no doubt it will be taken care of. Did you have any trouble finding us?"

"No, Sir. Aunt Ruth accompanied me this morning and everyone I've met has been ever so accommodating."

"Good to hear, good to hear. And you've been filled in the day's agenda?"

"Yes, Sir. 1:00 p.m. lunch, 7:00 p.m. dinner."

"I was thinking sausages for dinner. What do you think?"

"That would be wonderful," Beatrice replied. "As long as they come with onion rings."

"Of course they will." He looked up at the assistant, "Make sure we have lots of onion rings for this evening!"

"Yes, Sir," she replies.

"This afternoon, I want you to pretend you're a real customer. Pretend you're on a trip and need to take lots of gifts home." He reached into his side pocket and retrieved a stack of bills. Beatrice's eyes widened. As he handed them to her he said, "I want you to spend every last dollar. Request that all your purchases be taken to customer service so you can have your driver pick them up. This afternoon you can be anyone you want." He leaned in slightly, "Make up a good one, Doris and I would do this every time we took a trip. Some of the stories she came up with. I get the feeling you are kindred spirits. I'm sure you won't have any trouble."

"At the end of your day, I'll be expecting a full report. I want to know who gave you excellent service and if anyone gave you a hard time. Today, you are queen of Breckschnieder's and I want you to feel like you are treated that way. Any questions?"

"No, Sir," Beatrice replied. "I didn't expect this. I would like it to be my first day every day!" Fredrick Breckschnieder put his head back and let out a bellow.

"You're going to be great!" he said. "Tomorrow you are going to start in fabrics, Walt said you would enjoy that the most." Beatrice put her head down and started chuckling. "Anything wrong?"

"No," she said in between chuckles. "At times, Uncle Walter can be quite humorous."

"Good! I think we are all set." Fredrick was interrupted by a knock at the door. "Come in," he said.

"Sorry to disturb you, but you have another visitor," the plump secretary said in her deep gruff voice.

As she opened the door wider, there stood a tall, slim girl who looked to be Beatrice's age. She had long red hair that almost reached her waist. She wore an emerald green dress that made her eyes look twice their size, and her shoes had heals that made her at least two inches taller.

"Alma," Fredrick said. "Come in, come in, my dear." Fredrick walked over and gave her a gentle kiss on the forehead. "Perfect timing. Alma, I want you to meet Beatrice Miller. Beatrice is also starting today. Beatrice Miller, this is Alma Breckschnieder, my niece."

Beatrice reached out her hand in greeting. Alma hesitated and then reciprocated. Beatrice grabbed it firmly and instantly felt as if she could break it. There didn't seem to be bone in it and she held it out as if she was expecting it to be kissed or something. Beatrice had never shaken such a weak and lifeless hand. "Hello," she said. "It's a pleasure to meet you. Mr. Breckschnieder had mentioned that he had a niece that would be starting, I didn't realize it was on the same day." Alma smiled faintly but didn't say a word. "I'm sure we'll have plenty of time to get to know each other," Beatrice said out loud but it didn't' drown out another voice that whispered in her ear. It sounded very much like Uncle Walter. "Don't ever trust a weak handshake," it said.

Chapter Six

The Breck Building, as it was named, sat across the street from Breckschnieder's. It was an eight story building that had been renovated to house four floors of Breckschnieder employees and four floors of regular tenants.

As Beatrice entered, she was greeted by a short jolly man, whose ears seemed to be not quite centered on the side of his head. "May I help you?" he asked.

"I'm Beatrice Miller," she said.

"Welcome, Beatrice Miller, we've been expecting you. Bernard has already had your trunk delivered and you'll find it in your room." He turned around to the small mailboxes that lined the wall behind him. He reached into box 307 and retrieved a set of keys. He handed them to Beatrice and she held on to them tightly.

"You are on the third floor. Go down this hall until you see the dining room. On your right you will see the elevators. These in the lobby," he said as he pointed to the far side, "are for the apartments on the fourth floor and above, you can't get to your room on those."

"Down the hall to the dining room?"

"Yes. When you get there, you'll see the kitchen on the left, introduce yourself to Sade, can't miss her, she's the one in the apron."

"Thank you," she said. Beatrice walked down the long hallway. As she entered the dining area, she saw the elevator doors to her right and to the left was the kitchen. Standing in front of the stove was a short, stout lady wearing an apron. Sade was the staff cook. She was just shy of five feet and was about as wide as she was tall. She was a joyful soul who never spoke ill of anyone. When she smiled, her nose wrinkled.

Sade caught a glimpse of Beatrice out of the corner of her eye. She spun around and headed toward her, "Hello there, what can I do for you?" As Sade walked, she wiped her hands on her apron, just like Mother always did. There was a large stain of whatever was on the day's menu and it ran right across her tummy.

"I'm Beatrice," she said "you must be Sade."

"Well, Beatrice Miller, I've been expecting you." The two shook hands. Sade's hands were warm and gentle. "Did you stop at the desk and get your keys?" Beatrice held them up for inspection. "Your things have already been delivered, Bernard sent them over. Let me give you some instructions," Sade reached out her hand and took the keys. "307, that will be on the third floor to the right as you get out of the elevator. Breckschnieder employees are on the first four floors and you are to use these elevators. The floors above are actual apartments. Those residents use the elevators in the lobby." Beatrice nodded.

"My room is that first door you passed in the hall," Sade pointed down the hall where Beatrice had come from, "And the head clerk is the second door. You need anything, anytime, you knock on those doors." Beatrice nodded again. "If I'm not there, I'll be in here. Doors are locked at 10:00pm, you'll have to be buzzed in after that."

"Lunch is at 1:00 p.m.," Sade looked at the watch that hung around her neck, "You have just about an hour to get settled in." She handed Beatrice's key back to her. "Dinner is at 7:00 p.m., we all take turns cleaning up, you'll find the schedule on the board over there." Sade pointed to a section of the wall where a calendar, notes, advertisements and a few cards hung.

"Any questions?"

"No, not right now, but I'm sure I will by the end of the day," Beatrice said.

"Welcome to Breckschnieder's," Sade said wrinkling her nose.

Beatrice pushed the button on the elevator, the doors opened and she got in, when she turned around, Sade was back at the stove stirring a large pot that she could barely see into. Beatrice watched as the lights indicating which floor they were on lit up. When they arrived at three, the door opened and Beatrice exited, she turned to the right. At the end of the hall, she saw a white door with a small marker 307.

As she passed the other doors in the hall, she noticed each had its own personality. One had a little board where notes could be pinned; one had ribbons hanging from the marker. Number 306 had a *Do Not Disturb* sign hanging from the handle. "Hmm," Beatrice said, "Wonder whose that is?"

As she faced number 307, she put the key in the lock and turned the latch. It stuck but with a little jiggling, she heard the lock unlatch and the door opened. The room was larger than her room at home. It was long but narrow. Beatrice had been given an end room which meant there were windows on three sides. There was a white metal framed bed; it was made up with yellow and orange linens. There was a dresser with a small clock setting on it, a wardrobe next to the door, and two chairs that sat in the far corner. Beatrice walked over to the windows and looked down at the street below. "I'm not on the twelfth floor," she said, "But this will do."

Beatrice opened her satchel and carefully removed the decorations that had been made for her. She took each out and laid them across the bed. She opened the trunk and began putting her belongings away. She glanced up at the clock and without realizing it, an hour had passed. "Oh my gosh," she said. She grabbed her key and darted down the hall. As she waited for the elevator, she patted her pocket making sure that her spending money was safe.

Sade had prepared soup and sandwiches which were laid out on a table. A small line had already formed. She watched as each took a plate and bowl, chose their sandwich and Sade ladled their soup, each took a seat at the tables. Some were sitting alone, some in small groups. "Just like when we were in school," Beatrice said.

"Need a lunch mate?" Beatrice jumped. She felt a hand on her shoulder, "I'm sorry," said the kind and familiar voice. "Just wondered if you would like company on your first day?"

"Barnard, sorry I jumped, I guess I was somewhere else. Yes, I would love company."

"After you, my lady."

"Do you ever go first?"

"Not hardly," he said with a grin.

Beatrice noticed that people came and went during the hour. She assumed they were all on shift and their lunch breaks were staggered.

"Not everyone who eats here lives here," Bernard said as they finished up. "But once you live here, you are always welcome to have lunch here, even if you've moved out."

"So you lived here?" Beatrice asked.

"Yes ma'am, for the first five years. I loved living here."

"Why did you move?"

"Can't live here with a wife," Barnard said with a grin.

"You got married?"

"That's how I got a wife." Beatrice laughed. "If it weren't for Mr. Breckschnieder," Barnard shook his head, "Let's just say, the man has given me more than anyone ever has."

Bernard was interrupted by a stern voice coming for the serving line, "But we don't do that," Sade said. Beatrice turned her head. Standing in front of Sade was the girl she had met this morning. "You eat what we prepare, if you don't like it, you don't have to eat here."

"But I don't like this, can't you make me something else?" Alma asked.

"No, if you don't like what we are serving, you will need to make other arrangements," Sade said.

Alma crossed her arms and as she turned away, flung her hair so it whipped around her.

"This is going to be interesting," Bernard said quietly. They watched as Alma walked down the long hall toward the lobby. "She's in the room next to you, you know."

"She's the 'Do Not Disturb' door?"

"She has that on her door already? She's been here a whole three hours. Yes, this is going to be interesting."

After lunch, Beatrice set out to spend all the money Mr. Breckschnieder had given her. Her first stop was the perfume counter.

"Good day, are you looking for a fragrance for yourself?" the clerk asked.

"No, I'm on a trip with my father, he is in meetings all afternoon and has sent me here to buy gifts to take home with us," Beatrice's secret life had begun.

"And where is home?"

"Virginia, we are from a little burg in Virginia."

"All that way?"

"Father does business all over the country. I travel with him most of the time."

"That's wonderful," the clerk said. Beatrice nodded in agreement. "So who is the perfume for?"

"My mother," Beatrice said.

The clerk showed Beatrice several beautiful bottles allowing her to smell each scent. Beatrice chose the blue glass bottle; the fragrance reminded her of the patch of Lily of the Valley that sprang up each summer next to their front porch. "Mother will love this," she said.

"Are you taking it with you?"

"No," Beatrice said, "Would it be possible for it to be sent somewhere so our driver can pick them all up at once?"

"Of course, Miss? I didn't get your name."

She hesitated, she hadn't thought of a name. "Miss Walter," was the best she could come up with.

"Miss Walter, I will have this sent to our customer service desk, your driver can pick it up there. Will we be charging this to your account?"

"No," Beatrice said rather abruptly. "I'll pay for it now." She reached into her pocket and retrieved the stack of bills.

The clerk leaned over the counter, "You shouldn't carry all that money in your pocket," she said quietly. "Why don't I walk over to the purses with you and you can choose one, it would be best if that was hid."

The clerk escorted Beatrice across two isles to where the walls were lined with handbags. "This is Miss Walter, she is in need of a handbag for herself. What would you suggest?" Within minutes, the clerk had chosen the perfect one, they completed the transactions and Beatrice was in possession of her very first purse.

For the next few hours Miss Walter bought gifts for her brother Samuel who was away at school, her sister Rebecca, who was an nanny in New York, her little sister Mary, who was being tutored at home, and her Aunt Penny to name a few. As the packages piled up at the desk, word was sent to Mr. Breckschnieder that a Miss Walter was visiting from Virginia and was spending quite a bit of money.

As his custom, Fredrick Breckschnieder made his way to the sales floor to personally greet such customers. As Miss Walter was pointed out to him, he smiled a bit larger than usual.

"Miss Walter," he said as he approached her, "It's so good to meet you, I'm Fredrick Breckschnieder and I wanted to welcome you personally to Breckschnieder's."

Beatrice was beaming with delight. "Very nice of you," she said, as she held out her hand.

"I trust you are finding everything you need?"

"Most certainly," she said. "Everyone has made me feel so welcome."

"Glad to be here." He reached into his pocket and took out a business card. He quickly jotted something on the back and handed it to Beatrice. "If there is anything I can assist with, don't hesitate to ask," he said, as he handed her his card.

"Thank you," she said as she took his card. As Fredrick walked away, Beatrice turned the card over; *great story* was written on the back.

When Beatrice had spent all but ten dollars, she made her way to Breckschnieder's office. The guard at the double doors recognized her and opened the door for her. She walked between the desks and stopped at the last one.

As the woman looked out from behind a stack of files, she said, "What can I do for you Miss Miller."

"I just need to leave this for Mr. Breckschnieder," she said, as she handed her the purse containing the ten dollars.

The secretary took the bag, opened it and looked inside. She pulled out the money and the business card. "Do you need these?" she asked.

Taking the business card, she said, "I'll keep this, but the rest belongs to Mr. Breckschnieder."

"The handbag is his?"

"Yes, it is. I didn't think I could ask them to leave it at the counter."

Beatrice turned and walked out of the office. The secretary took the handbag and walked into Mr. Breckschnieder's office. "Miss Miller left this for you; she said she couldn't leave it at the desk."

Fredrick took the purse and opened it. "Ten dollars; she spent everything but ten dollars?" He removed the bills and laid them on his desk. As he handed the bag back, he said, "Have this wrapped and sent over to Miss Miller. Tell her it's a bonus for a job well done."

Chapter Seven

After an adventure filled afternoon and spending all but ten dollars of the money Mr. Breckschnieder had given her, Beatrice returned to room 307 to finish unpacking and preparing for dinner. Summer was just beginning and the sun remained in the sky a little longer each day. At 6:55 p.m., Beatrice once again entered the elevator and headed down for dinner.

Beatrice looked around to see if she could spot Bernard, but she knew if he really had a wife, he wouldn't be there. Alma also seemed to be missing, that didn't surprise her. What did surprise her was the relief she felt by not seeing her. Beatrice sat with a young man who lived on the second floor and across from young woman she thought was about four years her senior, who lived just above her. As dinner came to an end, she couldn't help but think that everyone she had met so far, besides Alma, she knew she would make friends quickly.

As Beatrice exited the elevator, heading for room 307, she noticed a small package sitting in front of the door. It was a Breckschnieder's shopping bag and inside was her new handbag. She read the note out loud, *For a job well done, thank you, F. Breckschnieder.* Beatrice hugged the purse as she entered her room.

She finished unpacking her trunk. She found the perfect place for everything and had storage space left over. She took the decorations that had been presented to her earlier that morning and set them around the room. She moved each of the chairs that sat in the corner to windows on opposite sides of her room. After everything was in place, Beatrice Miller sat in a chair and watched as the lights of the city began filling the dark gaps.

An hour past before she realized. The city was dark, but it was not dead. There seemed to be just as many people walking around as there had been when she first arrived. She prepared for bed and snuggled down under the covers. She did not bother closing the drapes, she loved looking at the lights of the city through her windows. Even when she turned off the last light, her room was aglow.

Beatrice was up early the next morning as it was a full day. Immediately after breakfast she was to report for a fitting. Breckschnieder's sales women wore black dresses made from three designs, and depending on which department you were working, had a matching apron. Beatrice was waiting in the large fitting room when Alma walked in.

"Are you having a fitting this morning as well?" she asked.

"Yes, I can't believe they make us wear those god awful dresses. Looks like they've just come from a funeral," Alma said.

"You're not from around here, are you?" Beatrice asked.

"No!" she said with a huff. "I'd never be from around here."

Beatrice just smiled. Alma had an unusual accent. When she said words like god, it was very harsh sounding, almost as if she was holding her nose.

"Ladies, sorry I'm a few minutes late, I have a customer coming as soon as we open and needed to make a few alterations on their dress. So who would like to go first?"

"I will," Alma said, without giving Beatrice a first thought.

"That OK?" the woman asked Beatrice.

"Sure," she said. *I'd like to see you change her mind,* Beatrice thought.

"Alright, step up here," the woman directed Alma to a large box step and began taking measurements. "There are three designs you can choose from, which one do you like the best?"

"How would I know, are you going to show them to me?" Alma sneered.

"Haven't you had time to walk the store?" she asked.

"No, not interested," Alma said.

"Well then, hmm, let's see... before I finish with you, why don't you go out into the woman's dress department and take a look at the girls working. I'm sure you will see all three designs, come back here and we'll finish up."

"I have to come back here? Why can't you just get them for me?" Alma asked.

"Because, you were supposed to spend time on the floor yesterday and you should have been prepared this morning."Alma glared at the woman who smiled back and continued, "We are done here, I'll see you in a few minutes. Beatrice, come on up, I'm ready for you."

Beatrice stood and slowly walked toward the box. Alma remained appearing to have no intention of moving. "Off with you," the woman said, as she shooed her away. Alma finally gave in and stepped off the box. She flung her hair around, "And that hair, needs to be up when you return. Alright Miss Miller, step right up."

Beatrice took her position in the center of the box. "You handled that very well," Beatrice said. "But aren't you afraid she will tell her uncle?"

"Mr. Breckschnieder?" she laughed. "I would like to see her try." The woman took her measuring tape and measured from Beatrice's neck to her waist. "If he knew that she came to a fitting unprepared, she'd be back on the train home."

"Really?"

"Yes, he is a kind man, but he does not tolerate anyone who doesn't want to be here. Turn. He doesn't play games." She pulled Beatrice's arm out and ran the measuring tape from her shoulder to her wrist. "You're a petite little thing, aren't you?" Beatrice smiled and shrugged her shoulders. "I'm guessing you're almost the same size as Ruth."

"You've dressed Ruth?"

"Several times. She has great style. There's a lot of people that think style comes with money. Let me tell you, it doesn't. You can't buy style, you come with it. Just because someone has money doesn't make any difference, if they don't have style or taste, they just buy a whole lot of ugly." Beatrice laughed. "Just you wait, you'll see. People spend a lot of money here and sometimes you have to package up some of the ugliest outfits you can imagine."

"Why do you do it?"

"You mean let them buy it? Well, that's easy. Give them what they want. I'll try, I'll say something like, 'let's try to match this with something else' or 'did you see how that dress matches this...' but it doesn't help. They have money, they like ugly stuff, so that's what they buy." Beatrice laughed even harder. "You think I'm kidding, just you wait, you'll see."

"I'm ready," Alma said, as she burst back into the room.

"You'll have to wait, take a seat over there, it's Miss Miller's turn," the woman instructed. "Now, Miss Miller, which of the three designs is your favorite?"

"I liked them all, but my favorite was the one with simple lines, not a lot of ruffles, and had a very wide collar that spread out over the shoulder." Alma laughed from her seat.

"My, my," the woman said as she applauded, "That is the latest style. Not too many like it – well not just yet – they're getting used to it. Classic, it's a beautiful dress. You've got taste my dear, you certainly have taste." Beatrice smiled and Alma snickered.

From their fittings, Alma and Beatrice were taken on a complete tour of the store. They saw everything, from the prop room which held all the extra display fixtures, to the loading docks, to the kitchens and storage room of all five restaurants. Their tour guide and trainer Martha, was a woman who looked about Beatrice's mother's age. She spoke in a very pleasant tone and had a very gentle laugh. During the tour, for no less than five times did Martha need to excuse herself and go searching for Alma, who felt the need to be somewhere besides the tour.

"You have to stay with us?" Martha said each time.

"This is boring," Alma would say.

"I'm sorry you feel so, but it's expected that everyone is familiar with the store. Now, please stay with us, the next time I won't go looking for you."

"Promise?" Alma asked.

"Yes, I'll also inform the office that you did not complete your training today and you'll have the pleasure of doing it again tomorrow." Martha smiled at Alma and paused for just a few extra moments.

Beatrice bit her lips together to keep from smiling. *That's exactly what Mother would have done,* she thought.

"Now ladies, let's continue," Martha turned and continued the tour. As the lunch hour approached, Martha dismissed both girls, "You'll be expected down in fabrics by 2:00 p.m. I suggest you make your way to the Breck Building for lunch quickly. Do you remember where Fabrics is located?"

"Yes," replied Beatrice and Alma rolled her eyes.

"Good. It's been a pleasure," Martha said as she held out her hand to Beatrice. "And Alma," Martha turned and extended her hand, "I wish you the best of luck."

Alma spun around, flinging her hair around her and walked away. Beatrice bit her lips again. "She's going to be interesting," Martha said.

Sade greeted Beatrice in the lunch line. "How's the first day?" she said.

"Wonderful!" Beatrice said with a smile. "We've had our fittings and seen the entire store – have to be back by 2:00 p.m."

"Where do you get to start?"

"Fabrics," Beatrice said with a surprising level of excitement.

"Fabrics?" Sade asked. "I don't ever recall hearing someone starting in Fabrics."

"Not everyone has an Uncle Walter who thinks he's clever," Beatrice said.

"Uncle Walter?"

"It's a crazy story that I don't have time for, but it's all his fault," Beatrice said as Sade handed her a plate.

"I would like to meet this Uncle Walter," Sade said. "Not too many people who can make things happen at Breckschnieder's and don't even work here."

Beatrice laughed. "If I ever have a chance, I'll be honored to introduce you."

"I'm going to hold you to that," Sade said. "Now, go eat!"

Beatrice took the first open seat she passed. "This taken?" she asked the young woman sitting next to it.

"No, not yet," she replied.

Beatrice set her plate down and pulled the chair out, "I'm Beatrice Miller," pulling her seat in. "This is my first day and I have to be back by 2:00 p.m."

"I remember my first day," the girl said. "Martha give you the grand tour?"

"Yes," Beatrice said as she picked up her sandwich.

"Are you starting in woman's wear?"

"I wish!" she said. "Fabrics."

"Fabrics?"

"It's a long story and let's just say that Mr. Breckschnieder was told that I love Fabrics so that's where I'm starting."

"Do you?"

"Love Fabrics? No! Can't stand them. But you gotta start somewhere. I'm just hoping that once I'm finished there, I won't have to ever go back."

"Well, Miss Walter, do you work here now?" a man's voice said from across the table. Beatrice looked up as she took a bite. "I would have thought you were on your way back, where was it? Virginia. Did your driver forget you?"

Beatrice began to laugh. "Yes as a matter of fact. Forgot all about me and left me here. Father said I needed real life experience and will be back next year to pick me up."

"Oh, you are good!" he said. "I can usually tell the story tellers, but you were good. I think you could be trouble." He pulled out the open seat across from hers. "So is this your real first day?"

"Yes," Beatrice said.

"Got the tour?" Beatrice nodded as she took another bite. "Starting in stockings?"

"Stockings? People actually start in stockings? I'm going to kill him," Beatrice said as she shook her head.

"She's starting in Fabrics?" her lunch mate said.

"Interesting. Never heard of anyone starting there, but you have to start somewhere."

At 2:00 p.m. Beatrice Miller was standing next to the cutting counter in Fabrics. From her vantage point it looked as if she was in a sea of fabric bolts. It was a hundred times bigger than at the Mercantile. The fabrics were perfectly displayed; separated by fabric types and then color. It looked like a thousand rainbows spreading across the department.

Besides it being a universe bigger than Uncle Walter's, most everything else was the same. Everything Walter had taught her was being duplicated at Breckschnieder's. Even the cash register seemed the same. The more she learned, the more brilliant Uncle Walter became to her.

Five days later, as the women in Fabrics were saying goodbye to her, Beatrice actually felt sorry to be leaving. *Perhaps Uncle Walter knew what he was talking about,* she thought.

For the next week, Beatrice worked in the woman's department and Alma was by her side, or at least she was when she decided to work. Alma had a way of disappearing when there was actually work to be done and conveniently reappearing when it was time to ring up a sale.

By the end of her second month, Beatrice had worked in every department. "I don't think I know anyone who has done that," Barnard had said at lunch one day. "Every department in your first two months, you must have super powers."

"I love it," Beatrice said. "I love every minute of it. I don't think I'll ever tire of it."

"Well, at this rate you'll be running the place by next year."

"Do you think I could?" Beatrice said.

"You're joking, right?" Barnard said.

"Why, is that too soon?" Beatrice said as sincerely as she could.

Barnard sat back and folded his arms. "I must say, Beatrice Miller, if anyone could do it, you could. But I'm not sure it will be next year."

"That's okay, as long as it takes. I never want to leave," she said.

"Let's get you through your first holiday before you sign up for life," Barnard said.

"I can't wait!" Beatrice said with the giddiness of a child. "Aunt Ruth has told me all about it. I can only imagine that living it is far more exciting."

"That it is, that it is," Barnard said with a boyish grin.

"Christmas at Breckschnieder's, I bet being at the North Pole could not be any more exciting."

Chapter Eight

Beatrice's excitement grew as the holiday's approached. Aunt Ruth had told her of the beautiful decorations that adorned Breckschnieder's during the holiday. She has seen pictures and couldn't wait to see the real thing. Breckschnieder's became a fantasy land at Christmas. The windows told a story, each displaying a scene.

It was a huge undertaking. Everyone who lived at the Breck Building spent every evening preparing the displays. Large white drapes hung in the windows prevented anyone standing outside a sneak peek and igniting their excitement.

The decorations went up on Thanksgiving Day and everyone participated. Mr. Breckschnieder had all the chefs' work together to create a Thanksgiving feast like no other. Dinner was served in the two dining rooms on the fifth floor. Music played and everyone ate until they felt they could burst. As the meal ended, the entire staff reported to the main floor for last minute instructions. In the next eight hours, Breckschnieder's would become a winter wonderland.

Aunt Ruth joined Beatrice on her first Thanksgiving. They worked side by side and had a glorious time.

"He buys new decorations each year," Aunt Ruth said. "Each year it's a different theme, each year new decorations."

"What happens to the old ones?"

"He sells them to other department stores."

"He is brilliant!" Beatrice said.

"Just a little," Aunt Ruth said with a smirk.

"It's my sixth month anniversary next week."

"Has it been six months already? My, time certainly flies. Are you doing something special with your day off?" Ruth asked.

"I'm not sure. I thought maybe Mother would want to come for the day, but she's helping Father. I don't have time to go home. Do you want to spend the day with me?"

"I would love to!" Ruth replied. "Tell me what you want to do and I'll make all the arrangements. Should we see a play?"

"That would be wonderful. I've never seen the Nutcracker and I've always wanted to."

"You've never seen the Nutcracker? Oh, my dear, I've got to get you out more! The Nutcracker it is! We'll have lunch, do a little window shopping. A trip to the museum, a quick bite and then the show; we'll save room for a real meal after the show. Sounds like a perfect day."

"Oh Aunt Ruth, it sounds like the most *perfectest* day I could imagine."

"It's a date. What time should I pick you up?"

"Ten?"

"Ten? Are you going to sleep in?"

"I'll try."

"Ten it is. It will be our special day," Ruth promised.

The two walked through the store distributing silver glass ornaments that sat in clusters on the counters. As they passed the break room, Beatrice caught the image of Alma out of the corner of her eye. She was stretched out on the sofa with a pile of magazines at her side. Beatrice didn't stop. She rounded the corner and started climbing the stairs.

"Was that Alma?" Aunt Ruth asked.

"I'm not sure?" Beatrice responded.

"Not sure, or don't want to say?"

"How about both."

"You don't seem surprised?" Ruth inquired.

"No, not really. She's kind of like that."

"Really?"

"She can be," Beatrice said carefully.

"That's very interesting. If Fredrick knew, he wouldn't tolerate it. Has anyone told him?"

"That's the problem. No one wants to tell him. She's a different person when he's around. She's a shining star, but when he's absent, she's...well let's just say, she can be very difficult to handle."

"Something should be done," Ruth said.

"Give it some time," Beatrice said. "I'm hoping she'll come around. There's always hope, isn't there?"

"You are a special one at that; always seeing the good in people. It's my experience that people don't change. But I'll let you hope for a while longer."

Beatrice and Aunt Ruth reached the top of the stairs. Ruth turned around and shouted down the stairs, "Well, Fredrick, I didn't think I would bump into you tonight. Aren't you usually in the yard organizing the final displays?" Ruth put her finger up to her lips to stop Beatrice from speaking. She then pointed down the stairs, "Watch," she whispered.

In a flash, Alma darted out of the break room. "I'm all finished with that, what else can I help with?" they heard her say as she rounded the corner.

Ruth chuckled and Beatrice shook her head. "Yes dear, I'll give you a little more time but tigers don't change their spots and you're not doing Fredrick any good by not telling him. We'll play it your way for a while."

"Thank you," Beatrice said. "Can we get back to our job, please?"

"Yes, ma'am," Ruth replied. "Lead the way!"

It was the wee hours of the morning before the final touches were complete. While Mr. Breckschnieder called everyone together and thanked them for their assistance, the large white drapes were taken down. As tradition would have it, Breckschnieder employees were the first to view the spectacle. Ruth and Beatrice wrapped themselves up in the coats and made their way to the first window.

"Ruth, it's them!" Beatrice said. "It's the Nutcracker!" Ruth watched as Beatrice looked in each window and read the words that hung behind the figures. It told a shortened version of the story. Beatrice read each word. Fritz and Maria were life size and Godfather Drosselmeier was anything but handsome. The clock had been imported from Germany and Beatrice thought it could have been the real one. The mice, the soldiers and the Nutcrackers were brilliant in color. Ruth delighted in watching Beatrice's excitement.

The following week, on her sixth month anniversary, Beatrice found a bouquet of flowers outside her door. The note read; *Thank-you for all you do! F. Breckschnieder.* She picked them up and set them on her dresser then she headed down stairs to the dining room.

"Beatrice, you're up so early. Thought you would sleep in this morning," Sade said. "Are you joining us for breakfast?"

"No, not today, thank you. My Aunt is picking me up at 10:00 a.m. and we have the whole day planned. Saving room for an early lunch, but I'm sure it won't be as good as your cooking."

Sade's nose wrinkled in delight. "Such a girl you are, wish they were all like you."

"Can't have everything," Beatrice said.

"Ain't that the truth?"

"Have you seen Alma this morning? Wanted to wish her congratulations on her sixth months."

"Seen eye nor hair of her," Sade reported. "Is the sign on her door?"

"Yes, but I think it's always there. Thanks Sade, have a

great day!" Beatrice gave her a kiss on the cheek. "I'll be ready for your cooking first thing tomorrow."

"Off with you, enjoy your day."

"I will!" she said as she darted down the hall. Beatrice ran across the street and entered through the delivery doors. She walked onto the floor. The store was not yet open for business and it was her favorite time to be there. Everything was in place; all the fingerprints had been wiped away from the glass displays. Any light that had gone out the day before had been replaced during the night and the entire store glowed with anticipation. Beatrice made her way to the atrium. She had yet to make a wish in the fountain, she could never think of anything she didn't already have. As she looked up she was breathless, the beauty of the atrium would never disappoint her. Now decorated for the holidays, it was all the beauty she could imagine in one place.

"Isn't it time for your escort to arrive?" The voice startled her, making her spin around.

"Good morning, Sir," she said. "Aunt Ruth will be here at ten."

"She's excited about the day she has planned for you," Fredrick said. "We had dinner last evening. She is very glad you are here, Beatrice, and so am I. Walt was right, you are a natural. I wish I had one hundred Beatrice Millers in my store."

"I'm not sure if one hundred of us could work together. We may kill each other."

"I can't image you would. I can imagine my sales increase at phenomenal rates, though. That would be worth it!"

"Worth us killing each other - or having a hundred of us?"

Mr. Breckschnieder shrugged his shoulders, "Both, perhaps." They both laughed. "Do you come on the floor often before we open?"

"Almost every day," Beatrice said. "It's my favorite time of the day. Everything is new and fresh and sparkles. I think of it as my private, perfect world."

"It is my private, perfect world," Fredrick said. "And I am so pleased I can share it with someone who appreciates it as much as me. I wish Alma did."

"She will," Beatrice said without thinking.

"Will?" he said. "You see it too, don't you?" Beatrice didn't respond. "It always saddens me when I have to let someone go. I had so wished she would share my love for this place. It breaks my heart. But I can't change her; she will have to find her own life. All I can hope for is that she has learned something during her time here that will help her later in life."

"It would be impossible not to," Beatrice said.

Fredrick looked at his pocket watch. "Ruth is never late; you had better gather your things. Have a wonderful day, and Happy Anniversary. I am so glad you are here."

Beatrice couldn't help herself; she bounded toward him with arms wide open. Mr. Breckschnieder embraced her and kissed her on the forehead. "Anniversary hugs are acceptable," he whispered. Beatrice squeezed one last time before letting go.

Aunt Ruth was right on-time as expected. As the taxi slowed, she flung the door open and shouted, "Get in!" Beatrice dove into the seat and the driver sped away.

As promised, Aunt Ruth delivered a perfect day. Lunch was tasty, the museum was exquisite, The Nutcracker was more magical than Beatrice ever imagined, and dinner was delectable. As they road back to Aunt Ruth's house, Beatrice asked, "Why did you tell him?" Ruth turned her head. "You said you would give it time. Why did you have to tell him?"

"Tell who? What?" Ruth asked.

"Why did you tell Mr. Breckschnieder about Alma?"

"Honey, I never said a word. He brought it up last night during dinner. I could tell he was bothered by something but he wouldn't tell me. I had to force him. He takes these things so personally. How did you know?"

"He said something to me this morning. We met in the atrium and he just blurted it out."

"He'll handle it. He's done it many times."

"I don't want him to have to handle it. I see how much he loves that place. It breaks my heart to think that someone as retched as Alma is going to cause him heartache. I wish there was something I could do."

"Retched? That's a very strong word."

"Well she is! She is the most retched person I've ever met. She doesn't have a kind word to say to anyone. She only talks about herself. She never does anything and blames anyone if she is questioned. I hate the way she is. She makes everyone's life miserable."

"You've witnessed much more than you've let on."

"I guess - I just hate it! Why do people have to be like that? Why can't they see what they are doing to those around them? How do you get them to understand?"

Ruth smiled a bit too mischievously for Beatrice's comfort; she felt herself becoming uncomfortable. "Why don't you stay at my house tonight? We'll get you a taxi at dawn and you'll have plenty of time to prepare for the morning."

Beatrice agreed reluctantly. She wanted to know what Ruth was thinking and yet, something about it made the hair on her neck stand up.

The two entered Ruth's home and were mobbed by a flood of hairy, barking creatures. "Get comfortable, there's an extra gown in the guest room. Meet me in the parlor and we'll have a nightcap. Hot cocoa alright?" Beatrice nodded. "Sounds good to me, too. See you in a bit."

Beatrice changed out of her dress and slipped into the nightgown she found in the top dresser drawer. She stood in front of the mirror and couldn't help but remember the morning, now six months ago, that started her first day. As she gazed into the reflection, there was something different. She had heard of people talk of an aura, but never believed she had seen one. She was getting the feeling she was about to. Aunt Ruth's summons startled her. She took a deep breath and headed toward the parlor.

Aunt Ruth made the best hot cocoa. She used cream, not milk and shaved the chocolate from a block of dark chocolate she bought at a confectionary. It was rich, and thick, and chocolaty. She floated a large dollop of whip cream on top. It wasn't until Beatrice was twelve that Aunt Ruth added her secret ingredients; a sprinkle of red pepper. She only served it to adults and as she felt twelve was old enough to get a job; it was also old enough to have the 'real' stuff.

The fire was blazing in the fireplace as they both settled in. Ruth in her favorite chair surrounded by five furry dogs and Beatrice curled up on the sofa, covering herself with an afghan. Aunt Ruth's newest arrival, Fred, curled up in the crook of her leg and used her knees as a pillow. There was an unusual chill in the air.

"Now, about our problem," Ruth began. Beatrice felt a shiver go through her body. "You okay, dear?" Ruth asked. Beatrice nodded. Ruth took a sip of cocoa. "Our little problem. There are times that we can teach others lessons if they refuse to learn them on their own. I do believe you could teach Alma a very valuable lesson, one that everyone would appreciate her learning."

Beatrice took a sip of cocoa, Ruth had her attention. "And how do you suggest I do so?"

"Take a bully, lock him in a closet, and in the morning, you'll be amazed what emerges. Works every time."

"You've done this before?"

"Doris and I," Ruth had to pause to laugh. "Doris and I handled most of our problems with *doing away*."

"How many times have you – done away?" Beatrice wished she could look inside of Ruth's mind. Was she serious? Had she and Ruth really done such things? Ruth was a kidder, was she pulling her leg?

"Oh, too many to remember. Doris was great at it! Her job was to make them as comfortable and trusting as possible. My job was to find the confining place. With her coaxing, we would get them to enter on their own."

Ruth took a sip as she remembered. "A few times we had to force them, but mostly they entered on their own. We would close the door, or lid in some cases, and retrieve them in the morning."

Bea couldn't take her eyes off Ruth. This wasn't real, there's no way she would have done such a thing. Mother would know... that made it seem even worse. Was Mother involve in this. She always said Ruth could take care of herself, is this what she meant? It couldn't be. This is nuts..."You just open the door and let them out?"

"Oh, no no no no no, that would have been a waste of our time. It's in the morning when they are ready to listen. It's just before you turn the latch..."

"Turn the latch?" *Ruth, I get it. This is a joke. You can stop now...*

"How else would you keep them in?" Ruth said.

Crap, she's serious. I always knew she was the crazy one, but not this crazy...

Ruth continued, "Just before you turn the latch, that's when you have a long discussion. It's amazing how quickly they agree. After that, anytime they need to be reminded, all you have to do is pretend you're turning a latch on the door," Ruth demonstrated, "and they snap back to the kind, gentle person you know they can be."

Beatrice scratched her head. This didn't seem dangerous. It did seem insane. But there was something real about it. In fact, it seemed like an interesting idea. When children are bad you put them in the corner or send them to their room. Not so easy with an adult. Alma wasn't really an adult, she was a kid; a very selfish, immature kid. She flashed back to her conversation with Fredrick this morning; she would do anything to help him. If she could get Alma to change her ways, he won't have to deal with her.

"Doing away with her for one night? That's it? No one gets hurt? Right?" What was the saying? Worse yet, what was she thinking? Could she really pull this off?

"Of course not. Doris and I never killed anyone, at least that we knew of. It's just a way to teach them a lesson."

"Hmm," Beatrice said. It surprised her and even alarmed her that she could see the legitimacy of such an act.

"Just consider it," Ruth said. "Let me know if there is anything I can do to help."

"I will," Beatrice replied and she took another sip of cocoa. An image of she talking to Alma through a small crack in a door, instructing her of the proper way to interact with others flashed in her mind.

"He would be so pleased if she had a change of heart," Ruth said lovingly.

And that's all Beatrice needed to hear. She would do it for Uncle Walter, she would do it for Fredrick. No one would get hurt. She was warming to the idea.

Chapter Nine

Nora Szala was a prickly old lady. Nora lived in Budapest, Hungry and visited Breckschnieder's twice a year when she was in the states, once in the spring and again just before Christmas. Beth Cummons had always been assigned to Nora until this visit when in a hurry, she tripped on the stairs, fell, and sprained her ankle, putting her out of commission.

Mr. Breckschnieder immediately requested Beatrice be assigned to Nora. "But Sir," the head clerk argued, "She's only been here six months."

"On her first day, she accompanied Miss Walter around the store and got her to spend almost every dollar she had. I'm sure she will get Mrs. Szala to do the same."

Nora Szala spent tens of thousands of dollars each visit at Breckschnieder's. She was one of their best customers and nothing was denied her. Every department knew that when Nora entered, their department should be prepared for anything. There was actually a 'floor runner' whose job it was to anticipate where Nora would go next and to have the department ready for her arrival.

Beatrice accompanied her the entire day. They stopped for lunch at eleven and tea at two. As the day was coming to an end, Nora spotted three large blue and white vases, handpainted, and imported from India. They were the only ones of their kind and price was no object. Beatrice joyfully wrote up the ticket and handed it to the sales person.

Nora Szala's driver collected her at six. Beatrice escorted her to the side door and accompanied her to the car. "Thank you, my dear," Nora said as she sat down in the back seat. "Next time we'll spend two days, just you and me."

"I'll look forward to it," Beatrice said. She closed the door, waved and watched as the car drove out of sight.

"How did it go?" said a voice from behind her.

"I think it went well," she said, turning around to see Mr. Breckschnieder. "You know better than I, how did I do?"

"She spent more than her last two visits combined," he said with great delight.

"Good! If she's going to spend her money, she might as well spend it with us!"

"My sentiments exactly," Mr. Breckschnieder said. "Can I buy you dinner?"

"No thank-you, sir. I would like to go over her receipts and I want to make sure those vases we added at the end are packaged properly. Besides, we had lunch and tea, I think I'm set till breakfast."

Beatrice sat at the spare desk in the head clerk's office and sorted through Nora's receipts. Nora Szala spent more in one day than Uncle Walter saw in almost a week worth of sales. Beatrice should have been tired, but she wasn't. If Mrs. Szala unexpectedly returned, she would have the energy to work with her all night.

Beatrice went to the fourth floor and found the blue and white vases. A large green trunk had already been delivered to the floor and was ready for the vases to be packed. Beatrice looked at the trunk. *Done away, just for one night,* began to eco in her head. *Just one night, no one gets hurt, he would love if she had a change of heart.*

Beatrice checked the time. Dinner was being served. She darted across the street and through the front doors of the Breck Building. As she entered the dining room, she scanned the room for Alma. She was sitting along at a table by the elevators and she was almost done. Beatrice sat down next her. "This seat taken?" she asked.

Alma only looked up with a forced smile. Alma only

ever wanted to talk about herself, so that's just what Beatrice did. As long as Alma talked about Alma, the conversation continued. As desert was served, Beatrice mentioned that she could use some help packing a few vases and if Alma was willing to do so, she would be happy to buy her a drink at the pub next door before they began packing. Alma thought it was a good exchange. Actually, she thought once in the pub, she would allow Beatrice to pay and then find a reason to back out of the agreement.

Beatrice and Alma spent more than an hour in the pub and the one drink turned into three. Just before Alma requested a fourth, Beatrice reminded her of the task still waiting for them and taking Alma's arm, led her across the street.

As they entered the store, Beatrice guided Alma up the back stairs to the fourth floor. As they walked toward the room where the chest sat, her heart was beating rapidly and her palms began to sweat.

"Need any help?" The voice startled her.

"No, no we're fine. Alma's just going to help me with something and then we are going to our rooms. It will take just a minute." She kept walking, half guiding and half supporting Alma.

As they drew closer to the trunk, Beatrice felt a chill go though her. "This is for your own good," she whispered. Alma just laughed. "You're feeling no pain, aren't you?

That may be good; this may not bother you so much." Alma started singing *Christmas Bells,* Beatrice hushed her.

The green truck was now sitting in front of them. Beatrice opened the lid. "Alma, climb in and let's see if you fit." Alma giggled a girlish giggle and climbed into the chest. "Easier than I thought," Beatrice whispered. She knelt down and straightened Alma's dress. "You do fit. Comfortable?" she asked. Alma nodded and continued singing. "Pretend you are a package and we're shipping you to the North Pole."

"OK," Alma slurred. "Good night."

"Good night," Beatrice said as she closed the lid. Beatrice buckled the straps just in case Alma woke up and tried to get out. She also thought that if anyone came down during the night, they would assume the trunk was ready to go and wouldn't bother it. "This is for your own good," she said as she patted the top. She could hear the muffled words of Alma's Christmas Carol.

Beatrice contemplated staying in the store all night but knew that the front desk man would worry. She went down the back stairs and crossed the street just before the front doors were locked.

"Good evening, Miss Miller," the desk clerk said. "Out pretty late tonight?"

"Yes, we had a huge sale at the store today and I needed to check to see if it was being packaged. Have a good night." She walked down the hall and pushed the up button on the elevator. As she exited the third floor and walked toward her door, she passed Alma's room. Her sign wasn't on the door. Beatrice turned the door knob, to her surprise it wasn't locked. She slowly opened the door, half expecting to see Alma. The room was empty.

Beatrice had never been invited into Alma's room, she didn't think anyone had. It was a mess. Piles and piles of clothes covered the floor. She had a dressing table with a mirror big enough to see her entire self, from head to toe. The bed wasn't made and three of the four dresser drawers were open with garments hanging out of them. "The sign - where's that sign?" Beatrice searched and finally found it lying on a chair. She left the room and hung the *Do Not Disturb* sign on the door. If it wasn't there, people would wonder.

Beatrice went to her room and sat in the corner with the lights off; she watched the city go to sleep. She waited for an hour, hoping that everyone on the first floor would be tucked away for the night. She changed her clothes, prepared for the next day. Then she made her way back down to the front door and pushed them open. If she left she wouldn't be able to return. She entered Breckschnieder's through the delivery doors with no interruption from anyone.

She returned to the fourth floor and quietly made her way to the trunk. Alma had stopped singing and Beatrice could hear her snoring. She patted the top of the trunk. She found a soft sofa to sleep on in a dark display room at the far corner of the fourth floor. She didn't sleep much. If she did doze off, she was quickly awakened by the thought of Alma pounding on the lid. She checked on her several times through the night, but the trunk was silent. Finally, around 4:00 a.m. she fell asleep.

When she awoke, she could see daylight peeking though the display rooms. "Holy Shit," she said out load. She had never put those words together before but somehow they seemed appropriate. She made her way to the trunk and as she rounded the corner, she heard voices. "Shit," she said under her breath.

There in the center of the room was a blue trunk being loaded with three well wrapped vases. She hesitated. "Good morning, Bea," one of the workers said.

"Good morning," she replied.

"You're here early."

"I needed to check on...there was a green trunk down here last night. Do you know where it went?" Beatrice asked.

"A green one? Oh, yes, it was already loaded, strapped down and everything. It went out early this morning. I'm guessing it's on the truck heading to the ports. Is there a problem?"

"No...well...no...there isn't a...just wondering where... yah...ah...no, no problem. I was just making sure it was picked up."

"Sure was."

"Were you here when it was taken?"

"Yah, I thought it was for these vases, but it was all strapped and ready to go."

"Did you look inside?"

"No, it was listed with the Szala shipment. That's where it's going. No stopping it now."

"Thanks." Beatrice said. She turned around and headed back to the stairs. She felt lost. Without thinking she found herself standing at the head clerk's door. She knocked.

"Just a moment." Beatrice felt faint. She leaned up against the wall. The door opened. "Are you okay?"

"Yes, I'm fine. Well, actually I'm feeling a bit under the weather today. I don't think I can be on the floor."

"Take the day off, my dear. You had a long day with Mrs. Szala. We'll cover for you today."

"Thank you."

"Go rest, take a long walk."

"I'll make sure I rest. Thank you."

Beatrice went back to her room and sat by the window. The city was coming to life. As she watched the people on the street, she longed to see Alma walking past. *Where is she? Is she still sleeping? Did someone find her?* She envisioned Alma pounding on the lid and some strong sailor rescuing her from her trunk. *It would be her luck to find a prince charming, and she would never thank me.*

Beatrice put on her coat and gloves and decided to take a walk. As she walked past Alma's room, she stopped. The sign was still hanging on the door. *Was she in there? Was she sleeping? Should she knock? Too risky,* she thought as she continued to the elevators. Beatrice pressed the down button and waited. She entered the elevator and as the doors were closing a hand reached in to stop it.

"Going down?" the voice asked.

"Yes," Beatrice said. The doors opened again and Phyllis entered. Phyllis's room was on the opposite side of the floor from Beatrice.

"You working today?" she asked.

"No, I'm just heading out for a little walk."

"You deserve it," Phyllis said. "Sounds like you had quite a day yesterday." Beatrice nodded. "Let me tell you, Alma was pretty put out that you were chosen over her."

"To be Mrs. Szala's companion?"

"What else? She threw a fit when she found out and all day she did nothing but complain."

"Really?"

"Yah, she said she was leaving, said it several times."

"Well, I don't think anyone would mind," Beatrice said.

"No kidding." The elevator doors opened and Phyllis exited first. "Have a good walk," she said.

"Thanks," Beatrice replied.

Beatrice walked aimlessly. She looked at window displays of other stores. She stopped and peered into a few cafés. She kept seeing Alma's face, or the back of her head, once she thought she saw her coat. Around noon she hailed a taxi and a few minutes later found herself in front of Aunt Ruth's.

She rang the buzzer and immediately heard a chorus of barking began. Ruth's voice came over the intercom. "Hello, who's visiting this morning? Hush now, hush my darlings, I can't hear."

"Aunt Ruth, it's me."

"Bea, what are you doing here? Are you alright? I'll be right down."

Within seconds Beatrice heard the latch unlock. The

door opened and there stood Aunt Ruth still in her purple robe surround by her furry friends. "Come in honey. You're looking a little beige. Come in."

Beatrice slowly entered the house and after being greeted and receiving a sloppy kiss from each of the four legged creatures, headed for the kitchen. "What can I get you?"

"Can you make some hot cocoa?"

"Of course, dear. Are you hungry?"

"No, I don't think I could eat."

Beatrice sat quietly gazing out the window as Ruth prepared the cocoa. Sensing she may need it, Ruth made a double batch. She walked over to the table, sat the cocoa down in front of Beatrice.

She waited for Bea to talk. The silence seemed an eternity.

"I did it," Bea said finally breaking the silence.

"Did what, honey?"

"The *doing away*."

"Oh, is that all."

"Yes, that's all."

"I thought it was much worse."

"Well, I think it might be."

"Why? No, wait. Start from the beginning. I have always found hearing the whole story makes it seem much less terrifying."

"Oh, Ruth, I don't think there is any way to make this less terrifying."

"Trust me. Start at the beginning."

Beatrice told Aunt Ruth about Nora Szala's visit, about the three vases and green trunk. She told her about three drinks and walk back to the store. She told her about checking up on Alma during the night and falling fast asleep at four on the sofa. Then she told her of the blue trunk.

"Where's the green one?" Ruth asked.

"It's was already picked up and on its way to the ports."

"I see," said Ruth rather calmly.

"Did anything like this ever happen to you and Doris?"

"Once or twice."

"Once or twice? Don't you think that was important information?"

"Could be."

"What am I going to do?"

Ruth shrugged her shoulders. "You don't have a lot of choices." Beatrice took a sip of cocoa. "Perhaps I should have added some rum this morning." Ruth's didn't seem overly concerned.

"What did you and Doris do?"

"You mean when *doing away* turned into *letting go*?"

"Letting go? You never said anything about letting go."

"It happened a time or two."

"A time or two! Ruth, what am I going to do?

Ruth raised her hands in the air. She shrugged her shoulder again. "Whatcha' going to do?" She grinned and took another sip of cocoa. "I'm getting that gin," she said as she stood. "Want some?" Beatrice didn't respond.

Ruth poured a shot into her cup and then one into Beatrice. "This is the real good stuff," she said.

Bea took another sip, but couldn't tell any difference. "How often did this happen to you and Doris?"

Ruth thought back, "Two or three times, at least that's what I remember."

"I would think you would remember these times vividly."

"No, not really. Pretty easy to let them escape your

mind. They aren't the important ones, the ones that changed, now those are the ones to remember."

Beatrice couldn't believe her ears. How did this happen? How did she ever entertain the idea? What made her act on it?

Aunt Ruth slammed her hands on the table and scared the crap out of Beatrice. "You need a day out!" she said. "Come on, get upstairs, change those clothes and let's go. You can't help Alma now." Bea didn't move.

"Beatrice Miller, pull yourself together and get that lily white bottom up those stairs. I'll meet you down here in ten minutes. MOVE!" she shouted.

Beatrice forced herself to stand and slowly climbed the stairs. This wasn't happening, it couldn't be. She hoped that when she got back in the room she would wake up and it would all be a dream. She opened the bedroom door and pricked her finger on the lock. It started to bleed. "Don't think people can bleed in a dream," she said as she lifted her figure closer to see.

Aunt Ruth was at the front door impatiently waiting for Beatrice to emerge from the bedroom. Once she did, Ruth opened the door and whistled for a taxi. "Come on, come on. We have all afternoon, let's get a move on."

"Aunt Ruth, I don't think I can."

"Of course you can." Ruth waited for Beatrice to make it through the door, pushed the dogs back inside, then she turn to lock it. She tossed the keys in the air, caught them, and placed them in her bag. Ruth grabbed Bea's arm and pulled her down the stairs. She jumped in the taxi and pulled Beatrice in behind her. Ruth reached across and pulled the door shut. "Take us to the zoo."

"The zoo? Why are we going there?"

"Cause it's a beautiful day and there's a new lion cub that was born last week. I want to see it."

Beatrice sat gazing out the taxi window. She had to stop this! But how? If she said anything the story would have to come out. She would get Ruth in trouble. Fredrick would find out about his beloved Doris. This would kill Mother. And Uncle Walter, what would it do to him? There was no way out.

"Ruth."

"Yes, Bea."

"How far away is Budapest?"

"Budapest, Hungry?"

"Yes, that one."

"It's a long way away."

"How long would it take to send something there?"

"You mean like a big green trunk?"

"Yes."

She nodded slowly, "I'm guessing about three months."

"Hmmm."

Ruth reached over and patted Beatrice on the knee. "Don't worry dear."

Ruth, please make this better. Make this go away. Stop time, reverse it. Get me out of here!

I'm sure Mrs. Szala and Alma will get along swimmingly."

Beatrice couldn't help but laugh. Nora Szala and Alma Breckschnieder in the same house. That would be life time of punishment for both.

"She's her problem now. Anyways, you don't know for sure that Alma was in there." Ruth squeezed Bea's knee. "Let's go see some lions!"

Beatrice took a deep breath. She was right; Beatrice didn't know for certain that Alma was still in there. She may have been rescued. Certainly they check trunks going to Budapest, Hungry. She threatened that she was going to leave any way; maybe she used this as her chance. If she did come back, it would be Alma's word against hers. She hadn't made friends, no one would believe that Beatrice strapped her into a truck. Beatrice couldn't even believe it.

The taxi stopped at a light. A tall redhead crossed the street. Beatrice stared. She could be anywhere. There's nothing that says she is still in that truck. And if she was, Ruth was right, she and Nora would get along swimmingly, wouldn't they? "A match made in heaven," Beatrice said out loud. She chuckled at that thought.

"What did you say," Ruth asked.

"Nothing," Beatrice replied. "I don't know for a fact that she's in there. Maybe I saved Fredrick the pain of letting her go."

"That's my girl. There's the smile I love." Ruth squeezed Beatrice's hand. "Driver, take us to the front entrance."

 Beatrice looked over at Ruth. Ruth looked back, she shrugged her shoulders and wrinkled up her face, "Whatcha' guna do?" she said.

And that's how it started. Beatrice Miller had experienced *letting go* for the first time. It didn't go as planned, but it wasn't as scary as she thought it would be. And when it was all over, Alma was no longer a problem for Fredrick Breckschnieder. She had helped him in a way, she had let her go. Someday, she hoped he would understand.

The taxi came to a stop and Ruth paid the fee. The two women exited the cab with great anticipation. The sky was blue, the sun shone warmly on their faces, and there was a new lion cub waiting for them.

Chapter Ten

Shortly after Nora Szala returned to Budapest, rumors spread that her husband had lost his fortune. It would be a long time, if ever, that Nora Szala would return to Breckschnieder's. Fredrick had only mentioned Alma once to Aunt Ruth. He was heartbroken that she would have just left as she did and he wished her well. Beatrice imagined seeing her less and less, and as time passed, so did the memory of Alma Breckschnieder.

Beatrice continued to work hard and after only two years was promoted to head clerk. At the same time, Cousin Albert had returned to the Mercantile. Albert had worked for Uncle Walter prior to Beatrice. He left to fight in the war and upon his return, wanted to spend time seeing the country. He traveled for several years and then one day, Walter received a letter asking if there was still a place for him at the Mercantile.

Albert and his wife arrived a few months later. Uncle Walter took down the Mercantile sign that hung above the porch and replaced it with a new sign, Reis's. Everyone assumed that Albert would take over some day. Uncle Walter had asked Beatrice if she would ever want to return. She thought about it for weeks.

"I love the city too much Uncle. I don't think I could ever come back. But I am honored that you would consider me." She had said. "Can we move the Mercantile to the city?"

Walter laughed, "Don't think it would survive there. Besides, you have your own Mercantile, don't you?"

"Yes, I guess I do."

Life at Breckschnieder's changed over the past two years. The Breck Building was going to be renovated and all of its tenants were asked to leave. Aunt Ruth invited Bea to move in with her. It took some convincing, but Ruth finally talked Beatrice into it. "There's so much room here," she had said. "It's only me. You'll have a floor all to yourself, your own apartment. Besides, I'm traveling so frequently with Fredrick, the house will be yours most of the time."

As the head clerk, she was the last to move out. Ruth met her at the door that day with a small bouquet of flowers, "Here's to new beginnings," she said.

"It's sad to be leaving."

"But you're not really leaving, think of it as relocating," Ruth picked up a tightly packed satchel from the pile sitting at the door. "You've acquired a few things these past few years."

Beatrice looked around the room, "Difficult not to," she said. "Bernard will send someone over to collect the rest."

As Beatrice closed the door behind her, Ruth pulled a screwdriver out of her bag. "What's that for?" Beatrice asked.

"A little souvenir," she said. "307 has to go." Ruth unscrewed the door plate from the wall and dropped it into Beatrice's bag. "We'll take this with us."

The two women walked through the empty corridor. Ruth dressed in the newest fashion and Beatrice fashionably clan from head to ankle. Ruth glanced down at Beatrice's feet, "Dear, you have to do something about those boots!"

"They serve me well."

"Can't we find something that can serve you well and are pleasant to look at?"

"When you do, let me know and I'll purchase a dozen," Beatrice said with a laugh.

The two passed room 306. It had been two years since Alma disappearance. Beatrice recalled being surprised by the short investigation and limited questions that had been asked. The police had concluded that after the drinks in the pub, Alma took off with a new beau she had been boasting about. The story sounded very plausible to Beatrice. It was no matter to her where Alma ended up as long as she was out of her world and would not be bothering anyone at Breckschnieder's ever again.

"What will become of this place?" she asked as they approached the elevator. "Is Fredrick thinking of enlarging the store?"

"I guess I can tell you now, we finalized the plans late last week. I've talked Fredrick into converting this into a hotel."

"Really?!"

"Yes. A quaint little boutique, like you find in Europe. Small little rooms, designed with items that come from the store. Construction begins next month. What do you think?"

"I think it's brilliant! Why didn't you say something sooner?"

"You know Fredrick; he didn't want anyone to think he was forcing them out. He thought best that we wait till everyone had found a place to live."

"And I'm the last," Bea said. She pushed the down button and they waited for the elevator. Beatrice looked up and down the hallway one last time. This had been her first home away from home. It was her first apartment and she was sad to be leaving it.

As they exited into the dining room, Beatrice saw Sade in the kitchen. "Is she leaving?" Bea asked.

"No, thank goodness. She's moving over to the big building. She will be the new executive coordinator for all the restaurants. It's a big deal. It's a big promotion for her."

"Good for her!" Beatrice said.

"Come, I want to show you what we have planned." Ruth showed Beatrice how the new lobby was going to look and what was planned for the entrance. "Fredrick will be taking the top floor," Ruth said.

"He's moving?"

"Yes, I've finally convinced him to get out of that stuffy office."

"Office? What do you mean."

"You don't know?"

"Know what?"

"Fredrick has a little one room studio apartment behind his office. He's lived there ever since the store opened."

"He has not," Beatrice exclaimed.

"Yes, he has. When Doris passed, he was months away from opening the store. He asked William and I to help him clear out the house, some things we put in storage but most he gave away. He moved into his office as a convenience and hasn't found a reason to leave, until now. It's going to be perfect for him."

"So when he says Breckschnieder's is his world, it really is."

"Yes, it really is. But it's time. He needs a home not an apartment and I'm going to do my best to give him that."

"You're a good friend," Beatrice said as she put her arm around Ruth's shoulders.

"I try," Ruth said. "Did I tell you about the café?"

"No."

"We are putting in a cozy café. Just like you find tucked in the corners of Italy. You'll be able to enter it from the street."

"In the Breck Building?"

"No, we thought so at first, but decided it should go on the street level at Breckschnieder's."

"Do you think these city folks are ready for that?"

"We'll make them ready," Ruth said with a smirk.

Beatrice's belongings were delivered to her new address before noon and she and Ruth spent the afternoon getting her settled. Beatrice would have the guest room on the third floor. Ruth reattached the room marker outside her door. Room 307 was now found on the third floor of the 'Ruth Building'.

It took almost a year to complete the hotel. When it was finished it was beyond spectacular. Ruth watched over every detail. She worked tirelessly; she even turned down a few buying trips with Fredrick, concerned that in her absence, some detail may be missed.

"Are you ever going to marry him?" Beatrice asked abruptly one night during dinner. Ruth had just taken a sip of wine and almost spewed it across the table.

"What in heaven's name...what made you...why?" she stumbled out.

"You get on so well. Everyone you meet thinks you already are."

Ruth carefully took another sip of wine. "He hasn't asked me," she said.

"Well, would you?"

"I would consider it," she said.

"Have you ever discussed it?" Beatrice asked.

"No. No, we have not."

"Why ever not?"

"Doris was Fredrick's first love. When they met, he was a shy awkward man with a big dream. Doris changed him. She gave him life. I guess in some way he would feel that he is replacing her, and he would never do that." She took another sip of wine. "William did the same for me."

"But you are still young," Beatrice said.

"Age has nothing to do with it, my dear. My time with William was cut short, and if I had it to do all over again, I would! A short time of bliss in this world is better than a lifetime of security. William and I experienced a lifetime in a fraction of a life. What more do I need?" Ruth looked around at her surroundings. "He's not here to share it with me, but he is here. And besides, Fredrick and I have a relationship I would never want to change." Beatrice shook her head. "You'll understand someday, Beatrice." Ruth lifted her glass as if offering a toast. "While we are on the subject, what about you? Any prospects?"

"No," she said with a snort. "And I'm not looking either; way too much to do to have to worry about someone else? Life is to live and I plan to live it all!" Beatrice lifted her glass in agreement.

The day before the grand opening of the new hotel, Mr. Breckschnieder invited several hundred prominent guests for a tour and samplings from the café. All who attended were astounded by its beauty and detail. Gold framed mirrors adorned the walls. Linen imported from England dressed the beds. Vases, figurines, and tapestries embellished the rooms. No two rooms were the same and each had its very own bathroom. Many of the guests stopped at the front desk before leaving to make reservations. All wanted the opportunity to stay in the new hotel. It was clear that the hotel would be a great success.

After visiting the hotel, guests were escorted to the café. This created an even higher level of excitement as guests tasted Italian Espresso and French pastries. The coffee was served in small white china demitasse cups. The men in attendance chuckled as they brought the small cups to their lips, but once they got a taste of the rich coffee, topped off with a dollop of crème, they were hooked.

It was very successful day. Fredrick and Ruth invited Beatrice to join them for dinner that night. Sausages and onion rings were served in the fifth floor train car.

"A great success, my friend. A great success indeed," Fredrick said addressing Ruth.

"They loved it, didn't they? They all loved it!" Ruth replied. She reached over and took his hand. "I told you they would. Fredrick Breckschnieder you are a success." She squeezed his hand gently.

Fredrick could not hide his adulation. "In all my dreams, in all my planning, never did I see a hotel," he said.

"And when will you be taking residence?" Beatrice asked.

Fredrick hesitated. "He's going to take his time," Ruth said. "His apartment is perfect, Doris would have loved it."

"Yes, she would have," he said. "Wish she was moving in."

"She is there," Ruth squeezed his hand again.

Fredrick turned to Beatrice, "And tell me, how were things in the shop?"

Beatrice laughed, "You still call it a shop. It is so much more than a shop."

"Not really," he said. "So how was it? Did any of our guests make it over?"

"Yes, we saw many of them," she said. "We had a very good day. Receipts were up. It was a brilliant idea to have replicates of the hotel rooms on display. Many of the display pieces need to be re-ordered."

"That was your idea, wasn't it Bea?"

"No Auntie, it was yours. But thanks for the offer."

A waiter stood at the table and cleared his voice. "Excuse me Sir, there is someone here to see you."

"Thank you, send him over," Fredrick said as he took the napkin from his lap, patted his mouth and wiped his hands. As he stood he held out his hand.

Beatrice looked up. There standing at the end of the table was a man of medium height with a few extra inches around his middle. His hair was darker than any natural hair color Beatrice as ever seen and was plastered with hair gel. As he reached out his hand to greet Fredrick, Beatrice could not help but notice his long, yet manicured, nails.

"Hello, Mr. Breckschnieder, it's a pleasure to see you again."

"Did you just arrive?" Fredrick asked.

"Earlier this afternoon, took a bit to get settled in before I came over."

"And your accommodation?"

"They are perfect. Feel as if I'm home," he said.

"Let me introduce my guests," Fredrick said. "This is Ruth Burrmann." Ruth held out her hand. Beatrice had almost forgotten that Aunt Ruth had a last name. No one ever used it. "Ruth this is Aldo Bovet, our café manager."

"And this is Ruth's niece and my head clerk, Beatrice Miller."

Beatrice reached out her hand and as she looked up, she caught an obscure smile on the gentleman's face. "It's lovely to meet you," Aldo said as he kissed her hand.

"You as well," Beatrice said as she tried to retrieve her hand but with no success.

Aldo paused for a moment, gazing into her eyes. His smile was less then genuine. He kissed her hand a second time. Beatrice felt a shiver go through her.

Chapter Eleven

The hotel's grand opening was even more successful then it's premiere had been. The reviews in the newspaper gave it the highest rating possible. There were rumors that the new design genius of Mrs. Ruth Burrmann should gain her an award in design excellence. It was a perfect combination, first class hotel next to the largest and most admired department store in the Midwest. Guests could now spend days upon days at Breckschnieder's and stay right across the street.

Beatrice loved the hotel. Frequently, she would have to deliver a package to a guest or meet someone in their room for a fitting. Walking through the lush carpeted hallways, admiring the pictures that hung on the wall, stopping to smell the large fresh floral arrangements that sat on glass tables, in all its beauty she was always reminded of its former appearance. The empty white hallways and comfortable rooms; when she had first moved in she thought she was in a hotel. But compared to the recent transformation, its former appearance seems pale and empty.

Unconsciously, Beatrice was always on guard as she walked through the hotel. She was cautious when she entered the elevator, always aware of who was in there with her or who was waiting at the doors to join her. Ever since Aldo Bovet arrived, he seemed to show up in unexpected places at unusual times.

"Beatrice Miller." She heard her name called from the end of the hallway early one morning as she set a precisely wrapped package in front of door 610.

"Ruth Burrmann," she answered in a loud whisper. "Do you know what time it is?"

"Join me for coffee," Ruth said lowering her voice.

Beatrice adjusted the package, fluffed the bow and walked toward Ruth. "How about a cocoa?"

"Cocoa - no - that will never do. You must start your day with an espresso." Beatrice wrinkled her nose. "You don't like it?"

"What are you doing here so early? I thought you were still in bed when I left."

"Fredrick is moving in today, There's just a few things I want to check on, I'm also having groceries delivered, it's time for the man to eat food that isn't prepared in huge kitchens. Maybe he'll even start cooking for himself."

"Or maybe he'll ask you to do it for him," Beatrice said with a girlish grin.

"Mind your own business," Ruth said, "Now let's have an espresso and start the day right."

"Never tried it," Beatrice replied.

"What?"

"Shhhh," Beatrice put her finger over her lips. "It's early," she whispered.

Aunt Ruth hooked arms with Bea and the two sashayed down the hall. As they entered the café, Ruth felt Beatrice's hesitation. "Something the matter?"

"No, or at least I don't think so. Just wanted to see who was working," Beatrice said.

"I hope it's that doll Christina. I could eat her up. Cute as a button," Ruth said, as she pointed to a corner table.

A tall slender girl with long blond hair pulled back in a ponytail, emerged from behind the counter. She greeted the two, "Good morning ladies, how is your day going thus far?"

"Christina, I was just telling Bea that I hoped you were

here. Christina meet my niece Beatrice. Beatrice this is Christina, you two will get along like two peas in a pod."

Both girls smiled as they acknowledged the other. Ruth was right, she was as cute as a button; big blue eyes that twinkled in the morning sunlight. A smile that drew you in. "I've heard so much about you," Christina said.

"Don't believe everything my Aunt says, she's been known to..."

"Not just from your Aunt. You're very well respected around here. Everyone seems to know who you are, and there hasn't been a mean word spoken about you," Christina said.

"Well, thank you. How long have you been here?" Beatrice asked.

"Since the café opened."

"Are you enjoying it?"

"Yes," Christina turned to survey the room, "for the most part."

"Good, I'm glad. If there is anything I can help you with, don't hesitate to ask," Beatrice said.

"I knew you two would hit it off," Ruth said. "Now, let's have some coffee."

"Two espressos?" Christine asked.

132

"I'll have cocoa," Beatrice said.

"Oh, no, she won't. Two espressos with whip creme on each. We also would like two chocolate croissants," Aunt Ruth was almost giddy with excitement.

"They are still warm, fresh out of the oven."

"That's what I was hoping you would say," Ruth began clapping her hands in anticipation.

"Don't worry," Christina said. "If you don't like the espresso, I'll bring you a cocoa."

Ruth and Beatrice sat quietly as they watched the city begin to come to life. "This is a lovely view," Beatrice said.

"I think it's the best view in the building," Ruth said.

Their quietness was interrupted a few minutes later as Christina set two demitasse cups and two small plates down on the table. "Enjoy," she said with a sincerity that made them feel that not enjoying it would be a crime.

"I don't understand your obsession," Beatrice said as she examined the cups.

"You will," Ruth said with a smirk.

Beatrice picked up the small cup, "Do I stir it or something?"

"You don't need to," Aunt Ruth said as she took a deep whiff of her coffee. She took a sip. When she brought the cup down, a small speck of crème remained on the tip of her nose. Beatrice chuckled, but Ruth paid no attention. "Heaven. Pure heaven," she said closing her eyes and allowing the rich robust flavors permeate her senses. "Go on, give it a try."

Beatrice brought the cup up to her nose, she smelled it. It was different than anything she had ever smelled. Father made coffee early in the mornings. She tried it once, but it was not something she wanted ever try again.

"Go on," Ruth insisted.

Beatrice took a sip. It wasn't at all what she expected. The whip crème had begun to melt across the top, making a thin layer of sweet deliciousness. The espresso was dark and earthy. As it made its way over her pallet, she could taste nuts and berries. As she swallowed, there was a lasting resemblance to dark chocolate. Not the cheap stuff you buy for a dime. This was the real thing.

Ruth looked on. "Not bad?"

"Not bad at all." Beatrice took another sip - and she was hooked.

"Wait till you taste the croissant," Ruth said.

Every morning from that day on, Beatrice Miller visited the café well before Aldo Bovet showed up for work. She ordered an espresso with real whip crème and a warm chocolate croissant. On most mornings, Christina served her at the corner table where she watched as the city came to life.

Chapter Twelve

While unloading a shipment of flour, Uncle Walter hurt his back and Albert had sent word inquiring if Beatrice could come home for a few days. Mr. Breckschnieder was so concerned for Walter's wellbeing, that he offered to let Beatrice go for as long as she needed.

"I think a week will be long enough," she said. "I don't think I would survive any longer."

Beatrice loved her time back at Reis's. Albert had made great improvements and he and Uncle Walter were getting ready for another expansion. Besides remaining the same location, very little else was the same. Albert had even improved the back hall. Large brass hooks now lined the hall with personalized name plates above them.

Albert kept the old National cash register. Beatrice stood in front of it. She brushed her fingers across the top of it and grabbed the handle on the side. She felt the brass letters affixed to the wooden cash drawer. "Angel bells, I've not heard them in a very long time," she said. "I miss them."

Mother planned a gathering every evening while Beatrice was home. Beatrice saw every family member and school chum that was in town and each day, at least one person asked if she was returning for good. *This isn't home anymore,* she thought. *I'm a city girl now — and will always be.*

Uncle Walter recovered quickly and Beatrice eagerly returned to Breckschnieder's. Beatrice was sitting at her table early the next morning when Ruth entered. "Good morning, dear," she said as she leaned over and gave Bea a kiss. "Welcome home."

"Thank you, sorry I missed you last night."

"Not to worry. Tell me, how was your time back home?"

"It was nice," replied Beatrice. "Mother fed the entire town."

"That's your mother."

"Albert has made a lot of changes in the store. It was fun to be back, but," Beatrice paused.

"But it's not home, is it?" Ruth asked.

"No. It's not."

"You've grown up, Beatrice Miller. You have a life of your own now and there's nothing wrong with that."

"I know. Mother makes me feel like there is."

"Your mother has chosen her life and no matter how much she – bitches – she loves it, every minute of it. And don't think for a moment that she isn't proud of you. She may not tell you, but I know she is."

Christina arrived at the table and sat down two cups of espresso with whip crème and two warm chocolate croissants. "Welcome home! I figured you were having your usual," she said. ""I want you to try something," Christina set a small bowl of raspberry preserves on the table. "It's the perfect topper for the croissant."

"Decadent," Ruth said. She took the small spoon, scooped up some preserves, and plopped it on the croissant.

"Make sure you get a little of the chocolate with it," Christina instructed.

Ruth took a bite. She closed her eyes and bit her lips tightly together. "Oh, my heavens." Ruth grabbed the edge of the table as if she needed to hold herself down.

"Did you come up with this?" Beatrice asked. Christina nodded.

"What did Aldo say," Ruth asked.

Beatrice could not help but notice the instant change in Christina's expression. "Uh, he said it was good," nodding her head very unconvincingly.

"Mr. Breckschnieder will be in his office in about thirty minutes. Send this up to him. In fact, can you deliver it personally? He likes to see faces, not just hear names." Ruth took out a small card that had her name printed on the front and wrote something on the back. "Here, make sure this is on the saucer."

"I really don't know if I can leave," Christina said, as she looked around the empty café.

Ruth dropped her smile and locked eye with Christina, "Thirty minutes, Mr. Breckschnieder's office. Anyone having an issue with that can talk to me personally."

Christina chuckled, "If you say so," she said.

"I do."

Christina watched the clock and counted down every minute. As she prepared the tray she flipped over Ruth's card. *Meet the next café manager* was scribbled on the back. Christina's stomach knotted up.

When Christina returned to the café, Aldo was waiting for her and cornered her in the back room, "Where have you been?" he asked.

"Mrs. Burrmann asked me to make a delivery," she said.

"I bet she did," he said. "Where were you really?"

"I told you," Christina said sternly. "Mrs. Burrmann asked me to make a delivery. That's all. You can ask her if you don't believe me."

"I wouldn't trust that bitch's answer," Aldo reached out and stroked Christina's arm. "I have a delivery I want you to make."

Christina ducked under his arm and backed away toward the door. "We have customers," she said. "I need to get back out on the floor."

"You should have never left it."

As soon as she was in the doorway, she spun around hoping that there were people needing her attention. As luck would have it, two tables were waiting to be served. Aldo stood in the doorway with his arms crossed watching her every move.

Later that afternoon, Beatrice sat in her office reconciling the prior day's receipts when there was a knock at her door. "Come in," she said. The door opened slowly and Christina quietly entered. "Christina, what a pleasure. Come in. Have a seat." Christina took a seat and slumped slightly in her chair. Her left thumb rubbed the center of her right hand. "I take it this isn't a social call," Beatrice said.

"No." Christina replied.

"Did Mr. Breckschnieder spit your croissant across the room?"

Christina broke a smile. "Just the opposite. His response was even more dramatic than Mrs. Burrmann's."

"Call her Ruth. Only the newspapers call her Mrs. Burrmann. You know, I hadn't heard her last name for so long that when Mr. Breckschnieder introduced us to Aldo," Christina swallowed hard. "I had almost forgotten she had one."

"Miss. Miller, this might have been a mistake. I'm not sure why I thought I should come to you."

"It's Beatrice, not Miss. Miller. The reason you came is because we have become friends, you trust me and you know that I will help you in any way possible." Christina nodded. "Now, tell me what Mr. Bovet has done."

Christina's head jerked up. "I didn't say he did anything," she said as she grabbed the edge of her chair.

"Stay seated Christina. You didn't have to say it; I can see it in your expression. Now, what has happened?"

"He's really not done anything. It's what he says he is going to do. Every day he makes comments about us, as if we are dating. He's telling customers that I'm his." Christina cringed at the thought. "I can't say it's intentional, but he shows up in the strangest places - at the most unusually times. It's always when I'm alone. It's like he knows where I'm going to be. He just gives me the creeps."

"Me, too," Beatrice said.

"Really? Oh, I'm so relieved. Not that I would want anything to happen to you, I just thought it was me."

"It's not you." Beatrice sat back in her chair. "Give me a few days to figure out what to do. He needs to be done away."

"Done away? I would feel awful if he was let go."

"Dear, letting go is exactly what he needs. You leave it to me. Now, I'm going to send a message down to the our Mr. Bovet telling him that Mr. Breckschnieder is requesting your services for a special event and that you will be on my schedule for the next few days. That should give you a break and allow us... or me to figure out the best way to handle this." Beatrice rose from her chair and walked over to Christina. She placed her hand on her shoulder and gave her a gentle squeeze. "As far as the rest of your day, I would like for you to deliver one dozen of those gooey chocolate cookies to, what's your address?"

"126 Fourth Street."

"To 126 Fourth Street. Make yourself a mug of hot cocoa and you have my permission to add just a touch of gin – you'll love it. Put your feet up and find yourself a good book. That's an order."

Christina stood and held her arms out to embrace Beatrice. Beatrice Miller quickly stuck out her hand, grasps Christina's and gave it a firm shake.

Beatrice contemplated the situation for the next two days. She visited the café at different times during the day in hopes of observing Aldo Bovet in action. There was something about him. She couldn't put her finger on it, but she knew the moment he took her hand the night they were introduced.

Beatrice frequently took walks around the building when she was facing a challenge. She loved getting out of store and into the fresh air. She would walk the perimeter of Breckschnieders, gazing into the windows, listening to the comments of her fellow shoppers. She stood outside the cafe windows looking in. Out of the corner of her eye saw long red hair falling down upon a emerald green dress. *Alda*, she thought, *I've not thought of you for some time.*

Beatrice made one more round of the building and as she returned to the cafe windows the red head was gone and so was her memory.

"Nasty, he's just nasty," Beatrice explained to Aunt Ruth over lunch. "From the moment Fredrick introduced us, I wanted to run into the kitchen and put my hand in boiling water. He shows up for no reason. He sits and stares at his employees. Gives me the creeps, Christina too."

"Well, there's always an answer," Ruth said without changing expression.

Beatrice paused. They had not spoken of the incident since that day. "You mean.."

"Sure. Doris would have. Doris would have done it the day after she met him."

"Seriously?"

"Seriously! She never wasted any time."

"I don't have a green trunk."

"No, no green trunks this time." Ruth took a bite of her chicken salad from the luncheon plate that sat in front of her. She chewed for a few moments, than it hit her. Pointing her fork at Beatrice, "As luck would have it, there is a new double sided refrigerator arriving next week. The old one is just not big enough."

Beatrice picked up her spoon and pointed it at Ruth, "Go on," she said.

"The deal is that they take the old one out and dispose of it. I'm guessing our Mr. Bovet is just the right size."

Beatrice pondered the option. In a strange way leaving Breckschnieders in an old refrigerator seemed appropriate for Aldo. "Do you know when?" Beatrice asked.

Ruth pulled a small calendar from her purse. "Next...I know I wrote it down...here it is...Tuesday. Look at that, they are showing up before the café is open." Ruth looked up at Beatrice with wide excited eyes.

"Tuesday? ...before they open?" Ruth nodded.

"...she'll have to help me." Beatrice took a sip of tea.

"...don't know if she'll make it," she picked up the sandwich from her plate. She inspected it and then took a bite.

"...but I can't do it alone."

Ruth scooped up another fork full of chicken salad from her plate. She examined it. "Did you ever think of putting grapes in a chicken salad? Brilliant idea, what kind of mind does it take to come up with this stuff?" Ruth completed the bite. She closed her eyes and bit her lips. "Excellent," she said.

Chapter Thirteen

If Beatrice was going to let Aldo go, she would have to meet him at the café. The thought of meeting him alone made her queasy. She may even need to play his game; the thought of it made her actually sick to her stomach. There were only two things she needed to be certain of; the first, that only she, Aldo and possibly Christina were in the café before the new refrigerator was delivered. And second, that she had a sure fire way to knock Mr. Creepy unconscious. She certainly was not going to invite him to the pub for a few drinks.

Beatrice made an appointment with the Breckschnieder nurse. Fredrick insisted that there was a nurse present at all times in his store. "Between the number of employees and the number of customers, we can't take any chances," he had said. Three nurses were hired and remained since Breckschnieder's opened.

"Miss. Miller, who are you here for today?" the nurse asked as Beatrice entered the office.

"This time it's for me," she said.

"You? You've never been here for you. Come in, have a seat, what can I do for you?"

"I need something to help me sleep. Something that will put me out quickly," Beatrice snapped her fingers. "Once I'm out, I sleep like a baby, it's just getting there that I'm having trouble with."

"You're working too hard," the nurse said. Beatrice nodded. "I have something that should help. I seldom offer it as a first option, but I think you'll be responsible." The nurse walked over and unlocked the cabinet. She reached for a small bottle on the top shelf. She weighed out what Beatrice assumed was about an ounce and poured it into a small vial.

"Here, just a sprinkle of this in a cup of tea just before bed. I mean - just before. It's best the first time you take it that you are already in bed. We're never sure just how quickly it will take effect. For some its moments, for others it's instant."

"In tea?"

"Yes, it works like a charm when it's in a warm beverage. Tea works the best just before bedtime. Remember - be in bed because when you're gone, you're gone."

"Sounds perfect," Beatrice said. "I'll make sure I'm ready."

"Please check in with me next week. This is strong stuff and I want to make sure you don't have any problems."

"I'll check in. Thanks again." Beatrice took the vial and left the office. She walked though the hall squeezing it tightly. As she turned the corner she almost bumped into Aldo who was standing staring into her office. "Holy shit! What are you doing here?"

"Just seeing if you were in," Aldo said completely unaffected by Beatrice's startlement.

Beatrice threw her hand behind her back attempting to hide the vial. "What can I help you with?" she asked.

"Nothing," he said. Then coldly and emotionlessly turned and walked away.

Beatrice was inside the café at 4:00 a.m. Tuesday morning. She turned one light on in the kitchen and a small one over the bar. She looked up at the clock, "He'll be here at 4:30 a.m. and the delivery people at 5:00 a.m. I have a half hour to get him to drink his coffee, fall asleep and get him in the old refrigerator. Rope and tape, where's the rope and tape?" Beatrice searched the back-room. She found it shoved in the corner. "Who put you there?" she asked.

"I did."

She jumped. "What the...." She turned to find Aldo standing in the door way.

"I put it there," he said.

"You're early," she said.

"I could say the same."

"When Mr. Breckschnieder asks for my assistance, I take it very seriously."

"I bet you do," Aldo said, with that same disingenuous smile she saw when they first met.

"It's not like that," she said.

"What is it like?" he asked. "I bet the three of you have some wild nights."

"That's disgusting!"

"Why don't you show me what it's like," he said moving toward her.

She threw the rope to him. He caught it. "Shall we start with this?"

"Knock it off." She had to gain her composure, she had to regain control. She glanced up at the clock. 4:20 a.m. "I would love an espresso and I understand you make the best."

"That I do," he said.

"I would love one. Don't you start your day with one as well?"

"I usually wait till mid morning," he said.

Well that won't do, she thought. "How about this morning you break that rule and share one with me." She did her best to smile.

"If you insist. Let me turn on the heat."

Beatrice cringed, she felt sick. She walked out from the kitchen with Aldo close behind. She stood next to the bar watching Aldo's every move. He turned on the brass machine and caressed it's side, feeling for the boiler; it would take a few minutes to heat up. He retrieved a small bowl of whip cream from a small refrigerator that sat next to the bar. He ran his fingers through it, presenting it to Beatrice as if he wanted her to lick it off. Every move was calculated, he was like a peacock showing off his feathers. He kept looking at her and she kept forcing a smile. It was 4:40 a.m. before Aldo completed their beverages. Beatrice kept a close eye on the door; Christina should be arriving any moment.

"Chocolate croissants!" she blurted out. "I love your chocolate croissant. Aldo,"

"I like when you call me Aldo," he said.

"Mr. Bovet, would you be a dear and get me one from the back room? Please."

"It will cost you."

"I'll gladly pay you in a bite," she said. Aldo grinned and raised one eyebrow.

She held back a moan as Mr. Bovet walked into the back room. Beatrice reached into her pocket and firmly grasped the vial. She opened it and poured its entirety into his cup. She didn't have time to stir but reached for the bowl of whipped crème and threw a dollop on each cup just as Aldo emerged with a plate containing one chocolate croissant.

Beatrice picked up the two cups and handed Aldo his. "Here you go. Now do you sip or gulp?"

"Espresso is to be sipped."

"I'm feeling a little crazy this morning, let's gulp it! Come Aldo, let's break the rules!" Beatrice lifted the cup to her lips and gulped it down. She hadn't anticipated that it would still be hot. The whipped crème had helped a bit, but she felt her lungs and stomach tighten.

"You are crazy," he said. "It hasn't had time to cool."

"But that's what makes it exciting."

"Why, Miss Miller, you just may have a wild side."

"Yes, I do. Go on Aldo, it's your turn."

Aldo raised the cup and took a sip.

"NO!" Beatrice shouted. "Gulp it."

Shocked by Beatrice's outburst, he lifted the cup once again and swallowed what remained.

Beatrice waited. *How long is this going to take?* She watched him closely.

"Like what you see?" he asked.

4:47 a.m. – *Where is Christina? When is he going to fall over?*

"Pour me another shot," she requested.

"Two shots, not many can handle that."

"I can. Go on, fire it up again." Beatrice was interrupted by a tap on the door.

"What's she doing here?" Aldo asked. "Both of you, how interesting."

4:48 a.m. – *nothing's happening. I should have tested it. It's not working.* Christina tapped again and Beatrice went to let her in. The latch stuck. "I can't get it... come on... unlock...Christina, I can't get it!"

"I'll do it," Aldo said from the bar. "Here let me at it."

"No, I'll get it, you stay there."

"Woman..." That's the last word Beatrice heard before the thud. She spun around. Laying on the floor was a pile of Mr. Bovet.

"The lock – open the door!" Christina yelled from the other side of the door.

Beatrice looked at the clock 4:50 a.m. "Holy Shit!"

Beatrice forced the latch and the door opened. "What have you done?" Christina shouted as she entered the café.

"Hush. You have to help me get him into to the refrigerator."

"The refrigerator? Are you nuts?"

"Maybe, just a bit."

Christina stepped back and looked at her. "Are you really doing this?"

"Looks like it. No turning back now. Come on... we have... oh crape! Why did you have to fall out here? We have to get him back there now. You take his arms, I'll take his feet."

The two moaned and groaned as they tried to lift him.

"I can't do it!" Christina shouted.

"Then let's scoot him." Beatrice knelt down on her knees. "Get down here." She started pushing him toward the door.

"Couldn't you have had him fall over in the back room?"

"Next time," Beatrice replied. "We're lucky he didn't make it all the way to the door."

Christina reached out to help push and then withdrew her hands. "Is he dead?"

"Nope."

"Are you sure."

"Nope. But I don't think dead bodies are so flexible."

The two pushed, rolled and scooted Aldo Bovet across the floor. As they maneuvered around the corner, Aldo's head bounced from counter to floor to counter. It took both of them to shove him through the doorway and into the back room.

"How are we going to get him in there?" Christina asked.

"We can't lift him. I guess we'll have to roll him up? Open the door."

Christina opened the refrigerator door and to her surprise it was already cleaned out with the shelves removed.

Beatrice stood up to evaluate the situation. "There's no other way, we have to roll him in there."

They turned Aldo around and sat him up so he was facing the refrigerator. His head dropped causing him to fall forward. With all her might, Beatrice gave him one big push and his head and shoulders landed on the floor of the refrigerator. The two grabbed his belt and together found the strength to lift the rest of him in. They maneuvered the lifeless body around until only his legs hung out. There was a knock at the door.

"Oh God, who is that?" Christina said.

"It's the deliver guys. At least that's who I hope it is. Come on, get your feet in there!" Beatrice ordered, as if Aldo could possible, assist in some way.

Christina picked up one foot and then slipped, causing her to lose her grip and fall to the floor.

"Those damn shoes," Beatrice said. "Where are your boots?"

"I don't wear boots."

"You do now!" Beatrice folded, twisted, and shoved each leg into to refrigerator and slammed the door just as the delivery men wrapped on the door one more time.

"You go get it," Beatrice said. "Delay them a little; I have to tie this up."

Christina stood and brushed herself off. She patted her hair in hopes that it was still presentable and walked out into the café. She waved at the two men standing at the door. "Just a moment, just finishing up," she said, with the biggest smile she could muster.

She walked pass the bar and checked the cups that Aldo had prepared for the second drink. She heard the sound of the tape being ripped from the roll. "Are you almost done," she asked.

"Almost," Beatrice said.

Looking back at the door, she gave the cutest smile she could offer, "I'm coming. Be right there." She did her best to sashay towards the door. She jiggled the latch a few times, pretending it was still stuck. The delivery man forced the door open.

"You alright?" one of them asked.

"Why yes, just an early morning. Getting ready for the day. I was just getting ready to pour a few shots; can I interest you in a starter for the day?"

"You here alone?"

"No, my partner is in the back. She's making sure everything's ready for you."

"Ain't Aldo supposed to be here?"

"I don't...well he..."

"Mr. Breckschnieder asked me to oversee this morning." Beatrice emerged from the kitchen and held her hand out. "I'm Beatrice Miller, so glad to meet you." She shook both men's hands. "We are so glad you were able to take care of this so early in the morning. Do you have the refrigerator?"

"We do."

"Wonderful. The old one is all taped and tied just like we agreed upon. It's ready for you to roll on out of here."

"I offered these two an espresso to get their day started."

"Good, good." Beatrice went to the bar, poured the shots and collected both cups. She placed a dollop of whipped crème on each and then remembered the vial and powder. *Which one?* She looked around the room. *Did he use the same cups?* Beatrice took a step toward the men, she intentionally tripped and dropped both cups forcing them to spill onto the counter. "Oh what a mess I have made. Here now, Christina will make you a fresh cup." Beatrice looked around. "You two can go right ahead and get that old piece of trash out of here, roll in the new one and Christina will have your espresso ready."

Beatrice showed the two men to the back room and as they walked into the kitchen, she looked at Christina and crossed her eyes. Christina burst into laughter.

"You two have a lot of spunk this early in the morning."

"It comes with the job," Beatrice said.

The men stood evaluating the size of the refrigerator, the size of the kitchen door, and the distance to the front door. "I hope we can get it through," one of them said.

"Me too," Beatrice agreed.

They grabbed hold of the case and with a shove moved it closer to the door.

"Feels heavier than most. Are you sure it's empty?"

"Did it myself," Beatrice said.

"Why isn't Mr. Bovet here? We could use another set of hands."

"I may not be Bovet, but I have muscle." Beatrice squeezed in between the two men and began pushing with all her might.

The case inched its way through the kitchen door; once setting in the café, a large hand truck was brought it and the refrigerator easily glided across the floor, though the front door, and onto the truck.

"Are you sure the old one isn't sellable?"

"No!" Christina blurted out.

"We've had our challenges with that one. It's done. It just needs to go somewhere where no one will be troubled with it again." Beatrice involuntarily winked at the men. She wrinkled her nose in an attempt to disguise the wink. "It just needs to be *done away*."

Christina clapped her hands, "Let's get that new one in here, times a ticking."

The new refrigerator rolled off the truck with ease, barely fit though the front door, got stuck on a floor tile and almost didn't fit around the corner. As it round the last turn and disappeared into the back room, Christina and Beatrice sighed a great sigh of relief.

"You two have earned your coffee this morning. Have a seat and I'll bring it over to you."

The two men sat down. Christina brought over two freshly brewed espressos and Beatrice retrieved a fresh plate of croissants from the counter. As she set them on the table she glanced up at the clock, 5:30 a.m. *It had all happened in an hour. An hour…just an hour? How long did the powder last?* She had no idea. *Was he waking up? Would he be out all day? Would he ever come to?* Beatrice watched the clock tick away. As the delivery men finished their last sips, she stood and held out her hand. "Thank you both again for doing this so early in the morning. We have to get that new refrigerator hooked up and ready for the day and I'm guessing you two have a schedule to keep. Don't mean to hurry you off, but the day is just beginning."

Christina took the last two croissants and handed them to the men, "Take these with you." Each reached out and took a pastry.

Beatrice opened the door and leaned against it. "It's time to be going." She winked again.

The two deliverymen tipped their hats, said good bye, and left the café. Beatrice shut the door and locked it.

Both women stood and watched as the delivery truck's rear lights lit up and the truck began to roll away.

"There he goes," Christina said.

"Yes, we're letting him go."

"That's one way of putting it."

Beatrice put her arm around Christina and they continued watching until the truck was out of sight. Dawn had just broken and the street was beginning to come alive with activity. Neither of the two saw Ruth walk up to the door and when she knocked, they both jumped.

Beatrice opened it. "Good morning," she said.

"Good morning to the both of you." Ruth said. "Is that new refrigerator here?"

"Yes it is," Beatrice answered.

"How wonderful." Ruth clasped her hands in front of her. "And tell me, have we let dear Mr. Bovet go?"

"We have," Beatrice answered. Christina looked surprised.

"Delightful!" Ruth said. "Christina, pour us a shot with double whipped crème this morning. Any chocolate croissants left?"

"I believe so," Christina said a little reluctantly.

"Bring us a plate with a little of those raspberry preserves on the side. Such a wonderful morning."

Christina walked behind the bar and began preparing Ruth's drink. She looked over at Beatrice who was dutifully cleaning up the spilled espresso on the counter. As the espresso finished brewing, Christina topped with a dollop of whip cream and carried it over to where Ruth was seated.

"Come dear, come have a seat next to me." Ruth patted the chair seat. Christina made her way over and sat down.

"We need to discuss your promotion."

"My what?" Christina said.

"Your promotion, my dear, with Mr. Bovet's expected done away, we'll need someone to fill his position and I think you are just the person. I've already discussed it with Fredrick and he agreed that if Mr. Bovet ever left, you would be a good replacement. Well, Mr. Bovet has left us, and in such a timely manner. I see no reason why we should delay the process."

Ruth continued talking as Christina watched Beatrice clean off the counter and moved to the bar. Beatrice picked up a cloth and began polishing the ornate brass espresso machine. Seeing her reflection, Beatrice smiled and polished a little more. The street outside was coming to life as the daylight grew brighter. The baker stuck his head through the kitchen door and yelled "Good Morning! See we have a new refrigerator."

"Yes, arrived this morning." Beatrice replied.

Ruth was still talking when the first guest entered the cafe. Without hesitation, Christina got up from her seat, greeted the customer, took their order, and began brewing their espresso.

"She's a natural," Ruth said.

Chapter Fourteen

Two Thanksgivings had passed since Christina had become manager of the café. Mr. Bovet was never seen again. Shortly after letting him go, a courier service had arrived to collect his personal belongings. Christina rang for Beatrice to come to the café after she directed the men to where Mr. Bovet had been staying. Both waited anxiously for information to be offered but none was.

Aunt Ruth renovated the brownstone earlier that summer. She had allowed Beatrice to choose all new furniture and wall colors. They added a small kitchen to the third floor making it a real apartment for Beatrice. At the top of the stairs, Beatrice hung four brass ornate hooks which Mr. Breckschnieder found for her on a buying trip. Above them was an old shelf she had taken from the Mercantile. Beatrice finally had her hooks and shelf with personality.

Ruth had every inch of the first and second floors remodeled as well; all new appliances for the kitchen and new fixtures in the bathrooms. The carpet was removed from the second floor in hopes it would be easier to keep up with the dog hair. However, the fourth floor was not touched. William's study and library had always resided on the top floor. It was the only place in the house the dogs were not allowed. When Ruth was feeling down or just needed time to think, she would make her way to the fourth floor, snuggle into one of William's large overstuffed chairs, and wait. Being surrounded by his books and framed drawings of the buildings he designed, inspired Ruth. She never waited long, inspiration would show up and Ruth would charge down the stairs ready to take on the world. William would always be her muse. The fourth floor would be his floor for as long as she lived there.

During the renovations, Ruth had arranged to take Beatrice to Paris. Beatrice was away from Breckschnieder's for almost a month. Christina counted the days until her return. When it finally arrived, she met Beatrice for dinner in hopes to hear all the details of her trip. Sausages and onion rings were served in the corner booth of the train car were the two sat.

"Mr. Breckschnieder missed you," Christina said.

"I'm sure all ran fine without me," Beatrice replied with an assured smile.

"It ran, but I'm not sure fine is how we would describe it."

"Any real catastrophes?"

"No, a few near misses. I think we all were waiting for one." Beatrice chuckled. "So tell me, I want to hear everything. I still can't believe you got to go."

"Well, it rained every day."

"Every day?"

"Yes, every single day! By the second week it wasn't so bad, it was sort of expected. There was only one or two afternoons when it cleared up and the sky was blue for as far as we could see."

"That's a shame," Christina said.

"Actually, it seemed as if the city was meant to be overcast and raining. It somehow added to its charm. We took an umbrella with us whereever we went. The rain didn't stop people from walking the streets or sitting at the cafes. Oh, the cafes. Christina, you would have loved them. They were everywhere. Tiny ones tucked inside little allyways and huge ones, whose outdoor seating lined an entire block."

"Ah, I can't imagine."

"And people were there from early morning to late into the evening."

"That's wonderful," Christina rested her head on her hand. "Sounds like heaven."

"Heaven - with a lot of rain," Beatrice laughed.

"The buildings were amazing. The architecture, we don't have anything like it here. Everything is so old there; buildings that have been standing since the 1700s. It all has such character, such history. They kept referring to *Napoleon*." Beatrice lowered her head not wanting anyone else to hear her confession. "After our first day out, I went to the library to find a book on Napoleon; a book in English about Napoleon. The librarian just shook her head when I asked. I'm sure she thought I was just one of those crazy Americans. She found one and I sat and breezed through it, it helped a little."

"Where did you stay?" asked Christina.

"We stayed in a few different hotels, but my favorites were these quaint little rooming houses. All the guests ate breakfast together. The kitchens and dining rooms were, I guess you would say their basements, or at least it felt like that as you were walking down the stairs. And they eat nothing like we do." Beatrice looked down at her plate. "And the breads! Oh my stars, the breads. Every shape and size you can imagine. Bread and cheese, bread and smoked ham, bread and wine. We have to either learn to make it like they do or find someone in the city that does."

"What were people wearing?"

Beatrice held her hands up in front of her and her face lit up, "We saw everything. Really – everything. But when we were close to the fashion houses, the women were dressed to the hilt. The coats were scrumptious, huge collars that wrapped around the neck, and yards of material draping around the bottom. As the women walked, the coat made them look like they were floating. Tweed suits with long straight skirts and some of the more exciting jackets I've ever seen; belted at the waist, big buttons down the front."

"Did you buy any?"

"Ruth bought a lot. I did buy two suits and a coat. They are being shipped. Ruth said, if I were going to wear them, I couldn't wear my boots." Christina laughed. "I bought a pair of heels."

"You bought a pair of heels?"

"Yes, I did." Beatrice lifted her fork and pointed it at Christina. "But you'll never see me wear them to work." Christina laughed. "I told Aunt Ruth that they are for a night out, a night which includes a lot of sitting."

"What was your favorite part?"

Beatrice put her head back, "I don't think I could say," she said. "There was so much. We did so much."

"Come on, there has to be one thing that you loved."

Beatrice sat quietly revisiting the last four weeks she would never forget. "I loved having breakfast with the other tourists. I loved that we had to wear layers of clothes every day and once we were inside a building, had to peel them off because they kept them so warm. I loved walking down the sidewalks, looking at the people sitting at the cafes, drinking espresso or sharing a bottle of wine. I loved the rain. But most of all," Beatrice closed her eyes, her smile warmed Christina. "Most of all, would be having hot cocoa at the top of the Eifel Tower with Aunt Ruth – with or without the rain."

"Awe, I want to go so badly," Christina said.

"Okay, then lets!"

"What do you mean?"

"Let's! We'll tell Mr. Breckschnieder that we want to go on a buying trip. And the next time a group is going to Paris, we would like to be considered to go along."

"Do you think he would consider it?"

"There's no harm in asking. It makes sense that you go because of the café, and I'm sure I could come up with a list of clients that would like me to do some personal shopping for them. The worst he could say is no."

As a matter of fact, Mr. Breckschnieder thought it a wonderful idea and made a note of it on next year's calendar.

Beatrice Miller was the center of attention for the next two weeks as all her customers listened to the details of the trip. Those who had been to Paris added their own stories and those who were still waiting their turn, imagined that they had gone with Beatrice.

Beatrice kept note of those customers who requested her to be their personal shopper on the next trip; Mrs. Taylor, Mrs. Bradshaw, Eileen Kramer, Mrs. Josephine Reynolds, and Mrs. Grace Marie Peterson, for whom she would do anything.

Chapter Fifteen

Grace Marie Peterson was the most refined, intelligent, and gracious woman Beatrice had ever had the pleasure to meet. She was of average height with curves in all the right places. When Grace entered a room, it lit up. She was charming, engaging, and above all, interesting. Beatrice thought her to have a natural beauty, one that didn't require a lot of make up or powders. Her hair was graying slightly but she wore it with dignity. She was everything Beatrice wanted to be.

Mrs. Peterson had three children. Her son was away studying law, and the two girls remained at home. Grace had been a favorite customer of Beatrice's since she started at Breckschnieder's. She had dressed her for countless events. She had dressed her daughters each year for the holidays. The Peterson's lived on the oldest street in town, in one of the oldest, and largest homes in the city. Each Christmas, they hosted the biggest gala of the year. The planning started in July, including choosing the attire for the family. Breckschnieder's was their Department Store of choice and Beatrice Miller was the only clerk they desired to work with.

Grace Peterson had a standing reservation every Tuesday and Friday in the Maple Room on the fifth floor. The Maple Room had one time been the woman's only dining room, but was now open to all. On most days, friends met Grace for lunch. Some days it was business aquaintances or women who shared Grace's passion for charity work. Rarely did Mr. Michael Peterson join his wife.

Grace Peterson volunteered every Wednesday at the local hospital. She chose the local hospital over the more prestigious one just east of town, because, as she put it, "These are real people." Grace did whatever was asked of her from holding babies to holding the hands of those who only have a few breaths left in this world. On Thursday, Grace had numerous committee meetings for all the charities she was involved.

"Why do you do it?" Beatrice had once asked her.

"I am fortunate," she had said. "Michael provides well for us. We have all we need and more. We both believe that it is required of us to give back to those in need. Michael works hard for his money and I work hard to make sure it's used wisely." Mrs. Peterson's answer made Beatrice only like her more.

While balancing the receipts one afternoon, Beatrice stumbled on a receipt for a woman's coat with matching scarf and gloves. It was charged to Mr. Michael Peterson and delivered to Miss Rebecca Smith, 723 Pine Street. Beatrice looked at the size of the coat ordered; it didn't match the size of either Grace or her daughters. With receipt in hand, Beatrice went in search for the salesperson who signed it.

Ada was the head clerk in the coat department. For all the wonderful words Beatrice would use to describe Grace Marie, she would use the opposite for Ada. Ada could be boisterous at times, she was very straight forward, never afraid of conflict. Beatrice wondered if she liked conflict just a little too much. But Ada ran a tight department and she ran it well.

"Beatrice, welcome back," Ada said as Beatrice walked through the doors.

"Thank you, Ada; it's good to be back."

"What brings you down today? Can't imagine you need anything new after your trip."

"I found a receipt for Mr. Michael Peterson, was he in yesterday?"

"Peterson," Ada paused for a moment. "Yes, Michael Peterson, a coat with a scarf and glove set, correct?"

"It appears so."

"I thought it odd, but she said Mr. Peterson had sent her in and that she was to charge anything she wanted to him."

"Was it one of his daughters?"

"I don't think so, she was about your age."

"Perhaps it was his secretary; I'll give her a call."

"Apparently, you think something's not right."

"Just following up, that's all. I'm sure there is no problem. Thanks Ada, have a great rest of your day."

Ada smiled and nodded. Beatrice left but not first without greeting the clerks on the floor. As Ada made her way back behind the counter, one of them approached her, "Something wrong?"

"Something smells a little rotten, that's all."

Beatrice phoned Michael Peterson's office.

"Good afternoon," the voice on the other end said. "Michael Peterson's office, how may I help you?"

"Good afternoon, this is Beatrice Miller from Breckschnieder's. I'm following up on a charge that was made to Mr. Peterson yesterday for a coat and accessories. Would you be able to confirm that for me?" There was a long pause, "Hello, are you still there?"

"Yes, yes I am. Would that have been sent to a Miss Smith?"

"Yes it was."

"I'm afraid it's correct."

"Will we be expecting any additional such charges?"

"God only knows," the voice said. "If that's all, I need to go."

"Thank you for your help, have a good day," Beatrice said.

"Good bye."

Beatrice hung up the phone, *that's odd*, she thought.

At that moment, Ruth stuck her head into Beatrice's office, "Come walk with me," she insisted.

"I'm a little busy," replied Ruth.

"Too busy for me?"

"No, never too busy for you." Beatrice left her desk and Ruth escorted her to the atrium. They stood looking over the fifth floor railings watching the activity below.

"I've finally convinced Fredrick that it was time for a face lift."

"But I like your face just the way it is."

"Ha!" Ruth said. "Not mine silly, here."

"A face lift, this is the most beautiful part of the entire store, there's not one thing wrong with it."

"There is nothing wrong with it, it just looks old and tired. It needs a new spark."

"I'm guessing Fredrick has approved?"

"Yes," Ruth said grasping Beatrice's arm. "We start next week. New fountain, the water will shoot higher and it has lights that change as the water does; a fresh coat of paint and a good polish on these old railings. It's going to take about three months."

"Three months? That's a long time for workers to be in the center of the store. It's going to create a mess."

"Well, look who has turned into miss puss. What's wrong with you."

"Nothing. I just stumbled onto something that makes me very uneasy."

"Tell me," Ruth ordered.

"Just a strange purchase charged to the husband of one of my dearest customers. I'm sure it's nothing."

"Sure of nothing! You're not sure. There are several reasons; it's a gift for a client, or a secretary, his wife, an aunt," Ruth pointed to herself and bounced her eye brows. "Or he's got something going on the side."

"He wouldn't do that," Beatrice insisted. "He has the most amazing wife, he wouldn't do that."

"Some of the most amazing women have been sent out to pasture for a newer, younger model. It has nothing to do with her, it's all about him. Selfish bastards."

"Such language," Beatrice said.

"It just pisses me off," Ruth said. "Selfish, self-centered, SOBs."

"You really feel strongly about this, sorry I brought it up."

"I hate that one person thinks they have the power to ruin so many lives."

"I can't imagine that he is like that."

Ruth rolled her eyes. "Well start, deary. They aren't all Fredrick Breckschnieder's."

Beatrice looked down onto the atrium. "When is work beginning?"

Ruth brushed her hair away from her face, folded her hands and placed them on the rail. "The painters come in next week. The fountain will be last, it will be torn up for a while."

She looked at Beatrice who appeared to be focused on the second floor. Ruth looked down. She saw a middle aged man, well dressed with an overcoat around his shoulders. He was standing next to a young woman wrapped in a white long coat with a scarf draped around the neck and a pair of leather gloves in her hand. They were talking and laughing like school kids. "Is that him?" she asked.

"Yes," Beatrice said softly.

"His daughter?"

"No."

"Certainly not his wife."

"No," Beatrice said. "What day is it?"

"Thursday, why do you ask?"

"She's at committee meetings on Thursdays making sure his money is handled well."

"Selfish bastard," Ruth said.

"Selfish bastard," Beatrice whispered. She wrapped her arms around herself, she felt chilled.

Chapter Sixteen

For the next few weeks Beatrice could not get rid of the nagging suspicion that followed her. Each day as she reconciled the receipts, she found herself taking second and even third glances on anyone whose name started with an M or P. "This is silly," she would tell herself. "There's nothing here." But there was and she knew it.

July quickly approached and Grace Marie Peterson had scheduled a fitting for the holiday gala; Tuesday at 10:00am Grace, her two lovely daughters and, to Beatrice's surprise, Mr. Peterson.

"So glad you were able to dress us again this year. I know your responsibilities have grown beyond fittings," Grace said as they entered the private show room.

"I will never be too busy to assist you," Beatrice said. "Looks like we may have grown two sizes since last year," she said to two giggling girls.

"Growing two sizes for them is acceptable," Grace said. "Let's hope I haven't."

Michael Peterson politely laughed, he leaned over and gave Grace a gentle kiss on the cheek, "You are as beautiful as the day I met you," he said.

Beatrice heard Ruth's voice in her head, "Selfish Bastard!" She shook it off. "Have a seat, she instructed. We've chosen a few examples to begin with, trust you will find something here that you like."

The ladies made themselves comfortable on the large upholstered chairs. Michael joined them. They would be seeing six models, one at a time, presenting six different designs which Beatrice had chosen. Each was as beautiful as the next.

"You're making this difficult this year, Miss Miller. They are all gorgeous!" Grace said after seeing the third model.

As the fourth presented herself, Beatrice heard a collective sigh. "I'm glad you like this one," she said, "it's my favorite as well."

"I don't think we need to see any more," one of the daughters said.

"Miss Miller has put together a collection, I think we need to see all the models," Michael offered.

"You're right Michael, we don't want to miss anything," Grace said patting his knee.

The next two models came out and although their outfits were exceptional, they did not compare to number four.

"Well, we have our decision. Alright, it's time for our fittings. Mr. Peterson, will you be staying with us?" Beatrice asked.

"Would that be a problem?" Michael asked.

"Yes, Father, it would," said the youngest daughter.

"Alright, I'll leave you ladies to it. Be back in a couple hours and we can have lunch," he offered.

"That would be lovely," Grace said.

Beatrice called for assistance and the three women were fitted for their gala apparel. Halfway through, Beatrice had arrange for a tray of delicacies to be brought accompanied by a refreshing beverage.

"You spoil us," Grace said.

"I trust I will be spoiling you for many years to come," she said.

Just before one o'clock, Mr. Peterson reappeared, ready to escort his women to lunch. "Miss Miller, will you join us?" he invited.

"No, thank you," she said. "I must get back to my work."

Grace walked over and took Bea's hands. "Thank you so much. You always make this day special for us." She pulled Beatrice close and kissed her as a mother would do.

"My pleasure," Beatrice said.

"Shall we," Michael said, as he held out his arm for Grace to hold. The four left the viewing room and headed for the fifth floor.

"There's nothing there," Beatrice said out loud. "Let it go."

Beatrice Miller was sitting at the corner table of the café watching the city come to life as Christina set her espresso on the table. "I met Grace Peterson's husband yesterday," she said.

"You did?"

"Yes, he was here with, I'm guessing, one of his daughters."

"Really?"

"It was just before lunch, just before twelve, I think. I didn't realize he had a daughter our age."

"I don't think he does."

"Really?" Christina's eyes fell toward the floor. "They sure seemed comfortable with each other. Maybe it was a niece or something."

"Perhaps," Beatrice said. Christina described the woman, it was not the same woman she had seen him with standing at the railing.

"She had a lot of packages. I got the feeling he had taken her shopping."

"Packages from Breckschnieder's?"

"Yes, I think they were all from here."

Beatrice heard Aunt Ruth's voice again. "Shut up!" she said.

"Sorry, I didn't mean..."

Beatrice reached out and touched Christina's arm, "I'm sorry, I didn't mean you. Just crazy voices in my head."

Christina stood to greet customers who had just entered the café. She looked down at Bea, "You okay?"

"Yes, I will be," she said.

That afternoon, Beatrice looked over every receipt from every purchase made during the previous morning. Ten receipts, all signed by Michael Peterson with the billing address sent to his office. Not one item was the right size or appropriate gift for his daughters.

Beatrice laid the receipts out on her desk.

Her mind flashed back to the phone call with his secretary. "Will there be more?" she had asked. "God only knows," was the response. "This isn't the first time, is it Michael Peterson? And I'm sure it won't be the last."

Beatrice tried to shake it off, but she loved Grace Marie Peterson almost as much as her mother. She couldn't stand by and watch her treated so. Michael Peterson needed to be shaken up a bit. He needed someone to rattle his cage.

From that day forward, Beatrice made sure she was available to greet Grace every Tuesday and Friday. She secretly hoped that she would see a change in Grace. She wasn't sure that it would be better, or worse, if Grace was aware of what her husband was doing.

Grace Marie entered the store each visit very much the same as the previous. She was elegant, charming, and gracious. "Beatrice Miller," she said, "What a delight to see you today."

Every visit, just the same; and with every visit Aunt Ruth's voice grew louder and louder.

Chapter Seventeen

Aunt Ruth, Beatrice Miller, and Mr. Breckschnieder stood on the fifth floor of the atrium looking down on the remodeling. All except for the first floor had been painted. The railings polished from both sides and the sky lights cleaned and restored.

"Ruth, I didn't think it could be more beautiful," Fredrick said.

"I agree," Beatrice added. "It's stunning."

"Why thank you," Ruth said. "I'm pleased."

"As you should be," Fredrick said.

"They will start the fountain tomorrow. Its going to be awhile. Our guests will be looking at a big deep hole for a few weeks, but once it is complete, it will be worth it."

"When is it expected to be complete?" Bea asked.

"It must be complete for the reception," Fredrick said.

"What reception?" Beatrice inquired.

"Your Mr. Peterson has reserved it for a reception next month," Ruth offered.

"He's not mine," Beatrice said with a hint of disgust. "Do you know what it is for?"

"He said for his staff, It sounded like an early Christmas party to me," Frederick said.

"He's paying a lot of money for it," Ruth added, "a lot!"

"If you need some assistance that evening, I would love to help," Beatrice said.

"Miss Miller, you don't do food," Mr. Breckschnieder said.

"Think it's time to give it a try," Beatrice said.

The following Tuesday, Beatrice greeted Grace as she entered the store. She escorted her to the fifth floor making small talk as they walked. As they entered the elevator, Beatrice asked, "Will you be attending the party?"

"What party is that dear?" Grace asked.

"Mr. Peterson is hosting a party in the atrium next month, will you be attending?" she asked again.

"I don't believe he has told me of that one. He is involved in so many charities and is out most of the week. When the children came along, I stopped attending many of them. That is why we continue to host the gala, it a chance for me to meet all those that Michael works with thoughout the year."

That's not all he does, Beatrice thought.

As the doors opened to the fifth floor, Grace Marie Peterson walked toward the dining room and Beatrice Miller went to her office. She pulled Michael Peterson's card and dialed the number.

"Michael Peterson's office," said the voice on the other end.

"Good afternoon, I am calling from Breckschnieder's to confirm the arrangements for the event Mr. Peterson has scheduled on the 20th," Beatrice said.

"Just a moment, let me get the calendar." There was a pause and then, "the 20th of when?"

"Next month."

"You must be mistaken; Mr. Peterson is out of town with his family that week. He has nothing planned."

"We must have the date wrong. Thank you..." Beatrice hesitated. "Could you leave word to have Mr. Peterson return my call? This is Beatrice Miller from

Breckschnieder's." Beatrice proceeded to give a return number, thanked her once again and hung up the phone.

The following day, Beatrice was handed a note that read, *Mr. Peterson rang, he will be in the café around 11:00 a.m. for a meeting, would be happy to speak with you then.*

Beatrice was sitting in the corner table at 10:55 a.m. Shortly after, Michael Peterson appeared at the entrance, he surveyed the room, removed his hat and walked toward Beatrice.

"May I join you?" he asked, taking the seat before Beatrice could answer.

"Certainly," she replied.

"You left a message for me yesterday," he said.

"Yes, I was checking on the final arrangements for the party," she said.

"Francine is handling all of that," he said.

"Francine, is that your secretary?"

"No, the party is in honor of Francine, I told her she could have it whereever she pleased and she said the Atrium at Breckschnieder's would be perfect. I understand it will be the first."

"Yes, it will. That is one reason we want to double check all the details, we want it to be a perfect evening."

"I didn't realize you handled events as well. You are quite a woman."

"We want to make it perfect, and Grace is such a valued customer," Beatrice said.

"Grace will be out of town that week, unfortunately," he said. "She's taking the girls to visit their brother."

"That's lovely, I'm sure they will have a wonderful time."

"Is that all, I'm expecting someone."

"Yes, that is all," Beatrice reached into her pocket and retrieved her card. "Here is my card, if there is anything you or Francine need don't hesitate."

"The personal card of Beatrice Miller, I'm moving up in the world." Mr. Peterson put the card in his pocket and took a table closer to the door. Beatrice watched as a young woman, a bit younger than her, entered. After spotting Michael, she smiled and walked toward him. He stood, glanced back at Beatrice and held out his hand in greeting. The woman looked surprised, but did the same, and sat down.

Christina walked over to Beatrice. "Is that the same one you saw him with earlier?"

"No," said Christina. "Different hair, different size, different everything."

Beatrice finished her espresso, took the napkin from her lap and patted her mouth. She stood, waved to Christina who was behind the bar and headed for the door. Without thinking, she stopped at the Peterson's table. "If you and Francine would like to have a preview of the evening, I can arrange that," she said with an inviting smile.

"That would be wonderful Michael," said the woman who was no longer nameless.

"Yes, of course. What night works for you?" Mr. Peterson asked

"What about next Wednesday? The painting will be complete and they will be finishing the fountain work. It may be a bit messy, but we'll make it special."

Michael reached out and took Beatrice's hand, she cringed, "Thank you," he said in an odd tone. "I knew you were someone I should know better."

Beatrice pulled her hand away gently as not to show her distaste. "Will 9:00 p.m. be alright?"

"That's late, but I think we can manage it."

Beatrice nodded and as she walked from the table, she heard the one now known as Francine say, "Maybe we can get a room here that night."

"Selfish Bastard," Beatrice said out loud.

189

Chapter Eighteen

Tuesday come and Beatrice met Grace Marie at the door as had become her habit. As she escorted her to the fifth floor, Grace confirmed that indeed they were making a trip with the girls to visit their brother, but this wasn't a girls trip, Michael was certainly joining them.

When they arrived on the fifth floor and the two parted, Beatrice made her way to the atrium. From the fifth floor, the hole for the fountain looked like a giant empty swimming pool.

"What do you think?" Beatrice jumped. "Or should I ask, what are you thinking?"

"Good morning Auntie, here for lunch?"

"Sure. You buying?"

"Don't have time today. Have a few things to take care of."

"Are you going to share? You've been in a different world for a few weeks."

"Oh, you know," she said.

"Someone needs a little awakening?" Ruth asked.

"Just a little," she said.

Beatrice woke early on Wednesday, but she was in no hurry to get out of bed. She knew that once the day officially started, it was going to last an eternity. She was meeting Michael and Francine at nine that evening in the Atrium. She had arranged with the dining room to have a light dinner prepared including four bottles of wine. She was having a small table and two chairs delivered from the fifth floor. There were candles and a side bar in the prop room where all the display pieces for the window displays were stored. She had an idea how the evening would unfold.

When she could put it off no longer, Beatrice threw the covers back and forced herself to sit up. She scooted to the side of the bed and allowed her feet to dangle off the edge. She sat staring at the floor. Grace Marie Peterson did not deserve to be treated in such a way, she saw no other choice and besides, Ruth was right, he was an selfish bastard. One final push and her feet hit the floor. She dressed, pulled her hair up and allowed a few ringlets to cascade along her face. She wrote Aunt Ruth a note: having dinner with Christina and plans after, don't wait up.

The hours ticked by slowly. Beatrice was never without tasks to fill her day, but today, it seemed as if none of them took up any time at all. She spent most of the day on the selling floor hoping time would move faster. Beatrice gathered her supplies from the prop room and set them behind the counter just beyond the Atrium. The table and two chairs were brought down around five and she met Christina at seven; as usual, sausage and onion rings were on the menu.

"You weren't at your table this morning?" Christina said, as she picked up a ring and took a bite. She pulled it back to inspect it. "Best invention ever!" She took another. "So, what's up? Where were you?"

"I stayed in bed a little too long."

"And..."

"And what?" Beatrice said.

"And....what's up? You're not exactly talkative tonight."

"Do you have plans later?" she asked.

"Why Miss Miller, are you asking me out? I noticed you're wearing your Paris shoes."

Beatrice laughed. She asked again, "Do you have plans?"

"No, but first are you going to tell me what's going on?"

"Well... it's just the Peterson thing, I hate it."

"What can you do about it?" Christina picked up another ring and dangled it in front of her face.

"I thought I could handle this on my own, but I think I need help."

Christina dropped the ring. "Go on," she said as she leaned forward.

"Mr. Peterson is expecting to have a preview of his party this evening. Francine will be joining him."

"You are on first name bases with Mr. Peterson's girls?"

"Not high on my achievement list."

"Apparently, it's an easy list to be on," remarked Christina.

"I need just a few minutes alone with him at the end. I've checked and there is a room reserved tonight for a Mr. Peter, I'm guessing it's the same. If you could help me serve them their wine tonight and then walk Francine to the room, it would be most helpful."

"I think I can manage that, as long as she is willing to go with me. We're not doing anything else, right? No big boxes or crates, just dinner and drinks?"

"Nothing else. After a few glasses of wine, I'm hoping they will be ready for anything."

"Where and when?" Christina asked.

"8:00 p.m. in the atrium."

"The atrium? It's a disaster down there."

"I know, if all goes according to plan, they will never notice."

"And if it doesn't?"

Beatrice bit her lip, her eyes widened as she took a deep breath.

Nine o'clock came and the two waited at the café door. Beatrice had arranged the table and two chairs in the atrium. Four bottles of wine, two glasses and a small plate of appetizers sat on the side car. A large candle lit the table and small candles in glass votives lined a walk way. A record player sat in the corner and was playing soft, inviting music.

Francine and Mr. Peterson arrived right on time. The two hostesses greeted the couple and escorted them to the atrium. The music and candles made the disorder of the missing fountain disappear. Beatrice poured the first glass of wine and began explaining what was in store for their party. After pouring the second glass ,she left the two alone. Returning a short time later, she poured yet a third.

"I'm not sure if I can handle three," Michael said.

"Don't worry, I'll get you a shot of espresso before you turn in," Beatrice said. Christina had to hold back her laughter.

By the end of the third glass Beatrice made her move. "Francine my dear, I understand you have a room reserved tonight. Christina will take you over and you can run a nice bath. I've made sure there are plenty of bubbles in the room." Francine giggled. Beatrice walked over and stood behind Mr. Peterson. She placed her hand on his shoulder, he looked up at her. "I have a few last minute questions for Michael."Michael felt a wave of excitement.

Christina helped Francine from her chair. "Come on, deary, let's get into a nice warm bubble bath." Francine reached out and grabbed the open bottle of wine. "Of course you can take that. And if you want, I can have some more sent to the room."

Oh, you are good! Beatrice thought. She remained behind Mr. Peterson, gently rubbing his shoulder as they watched Francine stumble out of the room. "She is delightful," Beatrice said.

Michael reached up and took Beatrice's hand. She wanted to pull it away; she wanted to hit him over the head with a bottle. "Have a few questions for you," she said.

"I have a few ideas for you," he said.

"You do?"

"How about you and me…"

"Tonight?" Beatrice asked. Michael quivered with excitement.

"Why Miss Miller," he said.

"I'm glad you understand." She walked around the table and took Francine's seat, she pick up another bottle of wine and began to pour.

"I don't think I should," Mr. Peterson said.

"But I haven't had any," she said. Beatrice poured a fourth glass for Michael and one for herself. "If you need an espresso after, we'll stop at the café." She wrinkled her nose and removed her shoes. She forced her toes to touch his ankles. Peterson chuckled.

"After?" he said. "Do you mean now? Here?"

"If you think we shouldn't," she said.

"Hell no!" he said, as he picked up his glass.

"I've always wanted to do it here," she said. "It's my most favorite place in the world. Here under the fountain." Michael turned around. He never saw the rubble, he didn't see the hole. He turned back around, all he saw was Beatrice.

"The store is empty," she said, "I made sure of that. You get comfy, I'll be right back. I've hidden a little something behind the pillar."

Beatrice took a slow sip of wine, blew out the candles with a long gentle blow. She slowly pushed her chair back, picked up a glass and took her leave. Michael was beside himself. He unbuttoned his jacket and threw it to the side, untied his tie and threw it in the other direction. Beatrice spied from behind the pillar. To her amazement, Mr. Michael Peterson stripped down completely. As she watched the silhouette of his naked body dance around the fountain, she put her hand over her mouth to stop her laughter. "You are no trophy, Mr. Peterson."

Beatrice prolonged her absence as long as possible. She had a negligee tucked away just in case. The thought of it made her sick to her stomach but if it was required, she would put it on. After watching Michael promenade one more time around the empty hole she knew it would not be required tonight. Michael Peterson would be a pushover if she showed up in a wool coat. Peterson danced around until the room started dancing on its own. He sat down on the edge of the fountain. Beatrice took a small vial from her pocket and poured it into the wine glass. When she emerged from behind the pillar, to Michael's delight, he saw three of her. She stopped at the table and refilled the glass.

"You're still dressed," he slurred.

"Not for long," she said, softly handing him the goblet.

"Oh, I don't think I..." Michael grabbed the glass and gulped it. He set it down on the edge, missing by about three inches and the glass shattered on the floor.

"I'm so sorry," he said.

"Not to worry. Here put your feet up on the ledge, we don't want any blood," Beatrice said. Beatrice helped him lift his legs. With every touch of his skin she wanted to scream. "Why not lay your head down, I'll get something to clean this up."

As soon as Mr. Michael Peterson laid his head down, he was out. Beatrice gathered his clothes and piled them by the door. "See what's it's like to wake up on display tomorrow, Mr. Michael Peterson." Then it hit her. "You shouldn't sleep out here in the cold."

Beatrice stepped over the ledge of the fountain. She pulled back the black tarp that covered the newly laid base. To her surprise, she felt sand. She knelt down and began digging a long, wide gutter. *I'll never build sandcastles again,* she thought. Once the trough was dug, Beatrice rolled Mr. Peterson's body off the ledge and into the sand. He moaned as he hit but never woke. She piled the excess sand around him and covered him with the tarp. "Nighty night," she said.

"Beatrice, where are you," Christina whispered.

"Over here. Almost done," she whispered back.

"Where is Mr...?" Christina paused, she walked over to the fountain edge. "You didn't!"

"He's all tucked in for the night. And Francine?"

"She never made it to the tub. I was preparing her bath when I came out she was fast asleep on the bed."

"Did you just leave her?"

"No. I undressed her, put her under the covers. She'll never remember a thing."

"Good."

"I added one little detail," Christina said holding her index finger up.

"And..."

"I left a little note..."

"A note?"

"Stating that he couldn't see her again and that she was not to contact him."

"Nice touch, how did you sign it?"

"M. P. I thought that's about all the sentiment he could muster."

Beatrice exited the fountain. She brushed the sand off her feet and put her shoes back on, "Here, help me move the table. They will be picked up in the morning." Christina collected the candles and the two moved the table and chairs to the door. Beatrice bent over to pick up Mr. Peterson's clothes.

"What are those?" Christina looked closer. "He didn't. You didn't?"

Beatrice pointed to her dress, "Does it look like I did?"

"He's naked?"

"Yes. Naked and enjoying the sands of Breckschnieder's."

"What will he do in the morning?" Christina asked.

"Hopefully go home to his wife," Beatrice said.

Beatrice and Christina made their way to through a dimly lit Breckschnieder's. Beatrice stopped and grabbed a large shopping bag from behind one of the counters. She recklessly shoved the pile of clothes in it and they continued to the café entrance. The store was quiet and dark except for a few table lights that remained on through the night. It had been a long day for both ladies and they were exhausted. Christina unlatched the café door and the two exited, as tired as they both were, they were very pleased with the outcome of the evening. Beatrice walked over and deposited the shopping bag in a trash can that sat on the corner. She then stepped out on the curb and hailed a cab, "Split one?" she asked.

"No, I'll walk tonight. Not too many warm nights left," she said.

Beatrice got in the cab and closed the door. Christina waved and turned to cross the street. Beatrice couldn't get the image of Michael out of her head and Christina replayed her and Frances's walk to the hotel room. Both were so preoccupied that neither saw the cement trucks pulling up to the back of the store.

Chapter Nineteen

Beatrice Miller was not sitting at the corner table as the city came to life for a second day in a row. She was snuggled deep under her covers when she heard the dogs sending Aunt Ruth off. She took her time getting up, even took time to make a hot cocoa.

When Beatrice arrive at Breckschnieder's, she entered through the delivery entrance, made her way up the stairs and down the hall to her office. She hung her coat on the hook, checked to see if there were any messages that needed her attention. She had only left a few hours earlier, nothing needed her at that very moment. She walked back out into the hall and started toward the atrium. As she rounded the corner, she saw Ruth standing at the railing.

"Good morning," she called out.

Ruth waved her over. "Come see," she said.

Beatrice did not change her pace. Assuming that Ruth was looking at a giant hole in the sand or even a naked Michael Peterson on display, she was in no hurry. She had seen more than enough of him the night before.

"Come on," Ruth shouted out. "Speed it up girl! Look what they did last night. It looks great!"

Beatrice froze. Eager for Beatrice to share her excitement, Ruth turned again, "What in heavan's..." she stopped, put her hands on her hips and said, "Why Beatrice Miller, you are an interesting shade of beige."

Beatrice forced her legs to move her closer to the railing. She grabbed hold and peered over. "Holy shit!" she said. "When did this happen?"

"They poured the concrete last night and the tile began going in early this morning. Look, they're spelling Breckschnieder in the tile. Do you like it?" Beatrice did not respond. "Beatrice Miller, I've seen that look before. Do you have something you would like to share?"

"He was there."

"Who was where?"

"There!" She pointed toward the fountain. "How long have you been here?"

"Just an hour or so."

"Did you talk to them?" Beatrice asked.

"First thing. They were pleased that the concrete was in and ready for them when they arrived."

"But they didn't lay the concrete, correct?"

"Beatrice Miller, what are you talking about?"

"Ruth, I done away with him last night. He was under the tarp in the sand...naked."

"Naked!" Ruth shouted, the words echoed through the atrium.

"Shhhh,"

"Naked?" Ruth said in a loud whisper. "You done away with someone but first you got them to be naked? Honey, you are the new appointed queen of letting go."

"Ruth, this isn't funny."

"Of course it's not, unless you are standing where we are."

"Not even then."

"I'm sure the men found him or poked him or uncovered him. They probably covered him up and sent him on his way. Naked, that's fabulous."

"But what if they didn't? What if he's still there?"

"Let him go, Bea."

"I don't think I can."

"Of course you can."

"But poor Grace."

"Poor Grace? Poor Grace? You did her a favor. She wasn't in a marriage, she was just employed. You don't know, he could be at home right now having tea and biscuits. And if he is still in there under the B R E C K S," Ruth threw her hands in the air, "whatcha' going do?" Ruth put her arm around Beatrice, "Naked. He was naked? Girl, you take the prize. Wish I had seen it."

Beatrice shook her head, "No, I don't think you would have. It's going to take some time to get the image of him dancing around the fountain out of my head. I'm not sure I will ever enjoy the atrium again."

"Dancing?" Ruth starting laughing so loud the workman looked up from the bottom floor. Beatrice put her hand over Ruth's mouth. Ruth pushed it away. "Dancing, naked in a dark atrium."

Beatrice bit her lip, "Naked dancing around the fountain in the dark." She broke a smile. Ruth was bent over in laughter. "Ruth, cut it out."

Ruth laughed harder. She crossed her legs. "You're going to make me pee," she snorted out.

Beatrice looked down at the fountain, the images of the night before played rapidly in her mind. Ruth's laughter seemed to be moving away and as she turned, she saw the back of Ruth, legs crossed, scooting down the hall toward the restrooms. Ruth would pause just enough to catch her breath and then the laughter would echo through the hall once again.

As Beatrice returned her attention to the fountain, she noticed Christina rounding the corner. Christina stopped and put her hand over her mouth. Beatrice watched. She surveyed the area. The table and chairs had been removed along with the side car and candles. She walked over to the fountain. Three workmen were laying tiles. She backed up attempting to see if the bottom was flat or if she could detect any large bumps. Beatrice saw a smile coming over her face. She covered her mouth once again, this time to prevent her from laughing out loud.

After a few moments of observing, Christina glanced up toward the atrium ceiling. She caught Beatrice out of the corner of her eye. The two women stared at each other, neither knowing how to respond. It was Beatrice who made the first move. She simply put her hands in the air and mouthed, "Whatcha' guna do?"

Their laughter echoed though the entire store.

Chapter Twenty

Autumn had arrived and Reis's Mercantile was turning fifty, Mother planned a fall celebration. The three city dwellers had purchased their tickets. It wasn't the most convenient time for Fredrick and Beatrice to be gone with the holidays quickly approaching, but it was Uncle Walter after all, they weren't going to miss it. Ruth had taken care of making their reservations and had somehow coerce the others to agree to arrive a day early to assists with the last minute preparations.

Rumors had been flying across the city as to Michael Peterson's disappearance. Some said he finally ran off with one of his 'charity cases', while others said business had taken him east. Beatrice had waited for Grace Marie that Friday morning, but she did not arrive. A messenger had delivered a request asking that the gowns prepared for the gala be sent to an address in Virginia. *Virginia?* Beatrice had thought, *I wonder if they will run into the Walters?* It saddened Beatrice to think that she may never see Grace again. She could only hope that the strong, gracious lady she had come to know could weather whatever changes had taken place.

Beatrice, Aunt Ruth, and Fredrick Breckschnieder boarded the train. Ruth had reserved a private compartment, and she and Beatrice sat across from Fredrick. Beatrice watched as the city passed her window and began to see farmland. It was the middle of harvest time and the fields were alive with activity.

"It's a whole different world, isn't it," Fredrick said. He was as engrossed in the scenery as Beatrice.

"Yes, a very different world," Beatrice agreed.

"I'm not sure who is picking us up." Ruth said.

"Walt is," Fredrick answered. "He's bringing the old truck."

"No, are you serious? We're all going to cram into that old truck?"

"Love that truck," Fredrick replied. "He's giving it to me when it dies."

"When it dies or he dies?" Ruth asked.

"When it dies, Walt's going to outlast both of us," Fredrick said.

"What are you going to do with an old truck?" Ruth asked.

"I'll find something." Fredrick waved his hand toward Beatrice, "Maybe we'll display it in a window." Beatrice laughed as she envisioned the old Mercantile truck in the Breckschnieder window. In a strange way, she could envision it.

"Lord help us," Ruth said. "There are times you are the most brilliant person I've had the pleasure of meeting and then other times, I don't know how you get through the day."

"That's why I keep you around," Fredrick said, as he leaned forward and patted her on the knee.

The train began to slow and Beatrice could see the station in the distance. She hadn't been home for some time and her excitement surprised her. Ruth reached over and held her arm, "Glad to be home?" she asked.

"I am," Beatrice replied. "It's going to be a fun weekend."

As the train came to a complete stop, the brakes squealed and the billows of steam erupted from beneath. The three city dwellers collected their things and stepped out onto the platform.

Uncle Walter was standing at the far end. As Beatrice stepped off the train, Uncle Walter put his fingers to his lips and whistled. Beatrice recognized it instantly and spun around. Uncle Walter waved his hands in the air. Beatrice pointed and shouted, "There he is!" She skipped a step and sprung into a full sprint right into Walter's open arms.

"It's so good to see you," he said, as they embraced.

"I've missed you so," she said.

"Me too, sweetie, me too."

Ruth and Fredrick where soon standing in their presence, but neither uncle nor niece were eager to let go.

"Walter, it's so good to see you again," Fredrick said as he held out his hand. Walter reached out keeping one arm around Beatrice.

"Glad you could come. Bea's mom has outdone herself for this one. I think she's enlisted the entire town." Beatrice loosened her hold. She moved to the side and hooked arms with Walter. If she had it her way, she would be by his side for the next two days.

"Hello Brother," Ruth said standing on her tiptoes to give him a kiss on the cheek.

"Glad you're here Ruth," Walter said.

A steward rolled a trunk and set it behind the small group, "Mrs. Burrmann, where would you like me to take this?" he asked.

"Is that for two days?" Walter asked.

"Never you mind," she said. "Where's that truck?"

Walter pointed across the way, "it's on the other side of the station," he said.

"You can take it to the oldest truck in town, you'll find it just over there, it has Mercantile painted on the side."

"Reis's," said Walter corrected.

"You've had it repainted?" Fredrick inquired.

"Looks brand new!" Walter said.

"I highly doubt that," Ruth groaned.

The four followed the steward around the corner, Walter and Beatrice arm in arm, Fredrick as excited as a school boy and Ruth shaking her head.

"Ruth, Ruth Miller," someone called from behind them. "Ruth, is that you?"

Ruth turned around. Standing at the entrance of the station was a middle aged man with thinning hair. "Ruth Miller," he yelled once again. "Rudy Meyer," he said pointing to himself.

"Rudy Meyer?" Ruth said. "Rudy, from school?"

"The very same," Rudy said now standing in front of her with his hand extended.

"Rudy Meyer," she said taking his hand. "It's been a long time."

"So long it's not worth counting. Ruth it's so good to see you. What brings you back?"

"It's the Mercantile's 50th Anniversary and my sister has put together quite a celebration from what I hear. What brings you back?"

"Mom's selling the farm and moving out west. Here to help with the sale," he said.

"West? California?"

"No, Washington. Her sister is there and they're planning on buying a little cottage together. It's actually a perfect solution for both of them."

Ruth's trunk had been loaded along with Fredrick and Beatrice's satchels, Walter handed Fredrick the keys and he was sitting in the driver's seat, Beatrice in the middle, and Walter was standing at the open door. "Ruth, you coming?" he said.

"Be right there," she yelled back.

Rudy reached out and took her arm, "Can I give you a lift, I have a car right over there. It would be so good to get caught up."

Ruth looked up at him, and then back at the truck. "Rudy will bring me over, go on without me, I'll see you in a bit."

Walter saluted, climbed into the front seat and slammed the door. Fredrick stepped on the clutch,

turned the key and after a few moans and groans, the
old truck snorted a cloud of black smoke and began to
chug. Fredrick howled in triumph, put the truck in to
gear and the truck jerked forward. Beatrice clapped,
Walter shouted "hurray!" and Ruth took Rudy's arm as
he walked her to his car.

Chapter Twenty-One

As the truck bounced, backfired and rumbled down the road, Beatrice couldn't help but chuckle at Fredrick's delight. Mr. Breckschnieder never let his persona of professionalism down. Beatrice had seen him in casual settings, but he was never anything but Fredrick Breckschnieder. Today, perhaps for the first time, Beatrice caught a glimpse of Fred. *Fred,* she thought, *I've never even heard Ruth call him that.* She glanced over at him; he had one hand on the stirring wheel, the other out the window waving at each car that passed. *Yes, today you are Fred,* she thought.

Uncle Walter rested his arm across the back of the seat and the other resting on the open window. He kept patting Beatrice on the shoulder and when she looked over at him, he would wink and pat her shoulder again.

The short drive came to an end as Fredrick pulled into the reserved parking space next to Reis's. "Uncle, you painted," Beatrice said as she slid across the seat.

"It needed a face-lift," he said. "I have a few more surprises for you." He held out his hand and helped Beatrice out of the truck.

"It looks wonderful!" she said.

"Thanks, I'm pleased," he said.

"Walt, I like the new sign, really grabs your attention," Fredrick offered.

"Beatrice!" the voice came from across the street. "Hello stranger!"

"Albert – hello – it's great to be home!" she said.

Cousin Albert was standing outside a one story brick building with large display windows. There was large gold lettering that read, Reis's Clothier. "Uncle Walter, what's that?" she asked, pointing across the street.

"I finally did it, Bea. Come on, I want to show you." Uncle Walter took Beatrice's arm and crossed the street with Fredrick close behind.

Albert greeted her with a hug. "He's been dying to tell you, can't believe he's kept it a secret," he said.

Walter held the door open and as Beatrice entered, her excitement radiated across the store. "It's beautiful," she said. Spread out in front of her was a small store filled with ready to wear clothing for men and women. It was as if he had taken a small sections of Breckschnieder's and replicated it.

"Walt, it turned out beautifully." Fredrick said.

"You knew about this?" Beatrice asked.

"Of course, he's only been talking about it for five years. Walt and Albert came to the shop when you were in Paris, we laid it out, placed a few orders, and Albert even spent time on the sales floor observing."

"Oh, I wish I would have been there," Beatrice said.

"So we did alright?" Walter asked.

"You did more than alright," Beatrice said. Beatrice walked through the aisles. There had never been a shop like this in her little town. Walter had even purchased a few mannequins and had them on display.

Three ladies walked into the store, "Good morning ladies," Albert said in a welcoming voice, "Welcome, how can we assist you this morning?"

Beatrice watched as Albert chatted with the women. He then called over a young sales clerk, made introductions and the clerk led them to the back of the store. "Have you been busy?" Beatrice asked.

"Yes," said Albert, better than we expected. "Everyone is pleased that they don't need to order from catalogs any longer, they get to see and hold the real thing."

Beatrice took Uncle Walter's arm. She squeezed it tightly. "I'm so proud of you," she said. "It's beautiful."

"That means the world to me," Uncle Walter said. "There's a few more surprises across the street."

"I can't wait," she said.

Albert escorted the three to the door and held it open for them. As he did, two more women entered. "Bea, we'll see you tonight. Your mother has put together quite the celebration and we're coming over to help this evening."

"Wonderful," Beatrice said. "Maybe we can find time to talk shop."

"Most definitely," he replied.

The three stood looking across at the Mercantile. The new coat of paint and bold sign reading Reis's brought new life to the place. "You've put little tables and chairs on the porch?" Bea said.

"Nice touch, Walt, how's the new menu going."

"New menu?" Beatrice asked. "You have a menu?"

"Come, I want to show you," he replied. They crossed the street arm in arm. As Beatrice climbed the steps to the porch, she was flooded with memories of her first day and the day she moved to the city.

"These steps have history," she said quietly.

"Good history," Walter replied.

There was a young couple seated at one of the tables. They had a road map spread out in front of them. As they discussed the trip that they were apparently on, each was refreshing themselves with a bottled soda. A young boy emerged from a side door with two plates in his hand; each containing a sandwich and a scoop of potato salad. He set them down carefully to their prospective owners. "Do you need anything else?" he asked kindly.

"No, thank you," the young man said.

"This looks delicious," his partner added.

"I'll be back to check on you," the server offered. He then wiped his hands on the short black apron that was tied around his waist. When he looked up, he realized he was being observed by an audience of three.

"Beatrice!" he said and ran over to her.

"William?" Bea said. The two embraced. "Mom never said you were working. When did you start?"

"It's only been about two or three weeks, right?" Uncle Walter said.

"Three weeks tomorrow," William offered with great pride.

"William, I can't believe you're old enough," Beatrice said. "My little brother, all grown up." She gave him another hug. "Who's cooking for you?"

Fredrick let out a laugh and Walter suddenly had a very boyish grin. "Do I want to know?" Beatrice said. "It's not Mother, is it?"

"No. I love your mother, but, uh, no. That would never work," Walter said.

"We've sent him a little help," Fredrick said.

Beatrice waited, but no one continued. "I guess I have to see for myself," she said, as she released William and entered the store.

The first thing she noticed was the corner where the hated bolts of fabric had once lived, was now lined with glass bakery cases filled with readymade salads, breads, pastries, and pies. The Mercantile no longer filled with the aroma of grains, seeds, dust, and dry goods. The air was filled with cinnamon, apples, and fresh baked bread. It drew her in, it made her mouth water. "Oh, my gosh," she said. "It smells amazing!"

"Good to hear," said a familiar voice from the kitchen. "It's got to smell good to taste good!" The cook walked out from behind the counter. She was just shy of five feet and was about as wide as she was tall and when she smiled her nose wrinkled. She wore a white apron that had stains right across where her tummy was. She wiped her hands in the same place.

"Sadel?"

"Well, Miss Miller. When you come to town, it's like royalty." Sade held out her hand in greeting.

"Sade, what are you doing here?"

"Mr. Breckschnieder," Sade began.

"Fredrick," Mr. Breckschnieder interrupted.

"Fredrick," Sade said reluctantly, "asked if I would be willing to make a trip to help your Uncle set up a kitchen and menu. I thought it would be a nice break, didn't know I would fall in love with it," she said leaning into Beatrice.

"It's easy to do," Beatrice said.

"Don't know how you left, girl," Sade said.

"Hey," Fredrick said as he put his arm around Beatrice, "Don't get any ideas, This one is mine for a while longer. Walt and I have an agreement, she's mine until he retires."

"We do?" Walter asked.

"Don't I get a say?" Beatrice chimed in.

"No, actually you don't," Fredrick said very matter a fact. Beatrice had worked for Mr. Breckschnieder long enough to know that he was not one to flatter. He was a kind man, but he was a strong business man first. He gave compliments only when he felt they were truly earned. Beatrice took great delight in being the object of attention. The idea that he was claiming her, was the greatest compliment he could offer.

"Sade, I just can't get over seeing you here," Beatrice said.

"Me either," she said. "But it's getting easier and easier," she said looking up at Walter.

Beatrice felt a slight spark between the two. "Does that mean you're staying?" she asked.

"She's on loan," Fredrick said.

Sade winked and wrinkled her noise. "We'll let him think that for a while," she said.

"You're very quiet," Beatrice said addressing Uncle Walter. Walter didn't say a word, he just stood there with a very satisfied grin. "You and I," Beatrice said pointing at Walter, "We're going to talk about this." She instructed. Walter simply laughed.

The conversation was interrupted by the laughter coming from two customers that had entered the store. Beatrice spun around, Ruth and Rudy were arm in arm.

"Rudy, I had forgotten all about that," Ruth said in between laughter.

"Hello you two," Walter said. "Take the scenic route?"

"We drove by Rudy's old house and the school yard. What crazy memories," Ruth said. "Sade," Ruth shouted as she came into view. "So good to see you." Ruth rushed over; Sade began wiping her hands on her apron. Ruth didn't wait; she reached around and gave her a hug.

"Mrs. Burrmann, I hoped to see you this weekend!"

"So, how is it? Are you having fun?" Ruth asked.

"More than I ever imagined!" she said.

Ruth looked up at Fredrick, "I told you, I told you it would be a perfect fit."

"Yes, dear, as always, you were correct," Fredrick responded.

"Come, show me your queendom," Ruth took Sade's arm and the two walked behind the counter.

"Not without me!" Beatrice said and Fredrick was right behind her.

"I'll just stay out here and tend to our customers," Walter said, but no one really heard him. Turning, he realized that Rudy was still standing at the door. "Can I get you anything?" he asked.

"No, no nothing for me." Walter walked behind the counter and Rudy came closer.

"So, are they partners?" he asked after a brief silence.

"Who?" Walter said.

"Ruth and him?"

"Fredrick?" Rudy nodded. "Mr. Breckschnieder and Ruth are very old and dear friends. In many ways they are partners," he said.

"But there's nothing between them, right?" he asked.

"Between them?" Walter paused, "That you will have to ask Ruth about."

"Where's my girl?" a voice said from the door way. "If I don't have her back at the house in ten minutes, her Mother is going to be on the warpath!"

"Father," Beatrice shouted as she came around the corner.

"There she is!" he said with arms opened wide. Beatrice ran toward him and he wrapped himself around her. "It's been too long."

"Father, it's so good to be home. Uncle's been showing me all the changes, I can't believe it. And William? You've let William work? I love it! He's so grown up. It has only been a year," she said.

"A very busy year," Father said. "And, a year is far too long."

"I know, I promise, never again," she said giving him another hug.

"We have to go; your mother has been watching the clock for the last hour. She can't wait to see you."

"Alright," she said, "Uncle Walter, I'll see you later – at the house?" He nodded. "If I can sneak away, I'll come back."

"Don't count on it," Father said.

Fredrick, Ruth and Sade emerged from the kitchen. "Fredrick," Father said as he reached out his hand in greeting. Fredrick walked over and took his hand. "Glad you could get away. I'm sure it's no easy feat."

"I wouldn't miss it for anything. Ruth's had our reservations for weeks and has been checking with my secretary daily to make sure the days were left open."

Father turned toward Rudy, "Excuse me, I didn't mean to interrupt."

"You don't recognize me, do you?" Rudy said. Father looked at him closer. "I'm Rudy,"

"Rudy Meyer?" Father said. "What brings you back?"

"His mother is selling the old place and he's come back to help with the final details."

"Mrs. Meyer is actually leaving," Father said. "She's been talking about it for some time."

"Yes, she's finally doing it. Never thought she would, but she's packed and ready to go," Rudy said.

"It's good to see you," Father said. "Ruth, are you coming?" Ruth looked at Fredrick.

"I'm going to hang out with Walt, if that's OK," Fredrick said.

"I assumed you would," she said.

"I'll be happy to be your driver," Rudy offered.

Ruth acknowledged Rudy and then briefly glanced back at Fredrick, "I guess I'm taken care of," she said. "You take that girl home and get her to work. I'll be there shortly."

Father offered Beatrice his arm, "My lady," he said.

"Why thank-you kind sir," Beatrice said. "William, we'll see you at home."

"OK sis," William said.

As Father and Beatrice walked toward Father's truck, Beatrice asked, "Do you know that Rudy well?"

"No, not well. Well, not any longer. We were in school together," Father opened the door for Beatrice. "Why do you ask?"

He shut the door and walked around to the other side. As he got in and put the key in the ignition, he looked over, waiting for an answer. Beatrice was looking out her window as Ruth and Rudy were stepping out onto the porch. Father waited.

"Just wondering," she finally said.

Chapter Twenty - Two

Mother was rearranging pots on the stove, moving the large one toward the back, making room for a new one in front. Steam was billowing out of another; the kitchen was a burst of aroma as Beatrice opened the door.

"There you are," Mother shouted. She threw her arms in the air and ran over to her. Beatrice was engulfed in her embrace. "I knew you would have to stop at the shop first, but you're going to have to share your time this trip."

"It smells wonderful," Beatrice said after letting Mother go. "What are you making?"

"Everything you can imagine. She's been working on this for weeks," Father said.

"Well, if this is any indication of what's to come," Beatrice said. "It's already a success."

One of the pots began boiling over and Mother raced back to turn down the heat. Beatrice walked around inspecting the rest of the preparations.

"Alright, put us to work," he said. Mother began giving direction and Father and Beatrice took their stations.

"Did you know that old Mrs. Meyer is leaving?" Father asked.

"She's been talking about it for years," Mother said brushing it off.

"I don't think anymore. You'll never believe who is in town," Father said.

"Who?"

"Rudy," Father said.

Mother slammed the wooden spoon on the counter. "Rudy Meyer is back?" she said. She began to laugh. "I never thought he would ever return."

"Why?" Beatrice asked.

Mother glanced over to Father. "No reason, Rudy was just an interesting guy, that's all."

"Well, he looks quite interested in Aunt Ruth," Beatrice said.

Mother laughed harder. "She's much too smart for that," she said.

"Seemed pretty taken to me," Beatrice said.

"Rudy Meyer is a woman's man. He's asked every girl in town to marry him at least once. That's why some said he moved, no one left to ask," Mother said.

"Where's he been?" Beatrice asked.

"Don't know," Mother replied. "Rumors have had him married several times. Mrs. Meyer never says much, just talks about his money!" Mother lowered her head and attempted to give her most seductive look, "Not his women."

"Well he's here, was at the station when we arrived and has been driving Aunt Ruth around ever since. He's bringing her here."

"He's coming here?" Mother said. "Don't worry my sweet, Ruth can handle herself."

"Let's hope," Father said just loud enough for Beatrice to hear.

"Enough talk about Rudy, we've people coming tonight and there's a lot to do."

"I thought we were celebrating tomorrow at the shop?"

"Tonight is family and a few close friends," Mother said.

"About thirty close friends," Father interrupted.

"Isn't that the entire town?" Beatrice joked.

"Almost," said Father.

"Enough already, we have things to do. Bea, you can start on those potatoes," Mother pointed to a bushel of yellow potatoes. "Please get those tables set up in the barn," Mother insisted.

"Already done, chairs and all." Mother gave Father her 'don't be an idiot' look. "Really, it's all set up."

"Give me the table clothes and I'll get those on," Father said.

Mother starred at Father who replied with a goofy smile. "I've lost it," she said. "I've finally lost it. I can't tell if you're serious or not." Father looked over to Beatrice and winked which made her giggle. She loved watching them banter.

"Beatrice, walk out with your father and see if it's set up."

"But I'm doing the potatoes."

"Why don't you come with me," Father said raising one brow.

"I don't have time for such nonsense," she said, as she snapped a towel at him.

The remainder of the afternoon followed suit. Mother gave direction, Father made it interesting and Beatrice peeled a lot of vegetable. Aunt Ruth showed up as Mother was transporting the food to the barn. She offered Rudy's assistance and Mother accepted. Fredrick drove the old truck around town before finally making his way to the house.

The evening was perfect. Uncle Walter brought all the pictures he could find of the early days of the Mercantile. One had Grandpa and Grandma Reis standing in front of the building surrounded by ten children. He also had the original papers from the purchase of the building.

Uncle Walter brought Sade. Beatrice thought it was wonderful. Cousin Albert was there with his wife and now four children. And every cousin that Uncle Walter had employed was either in attendance or had sent a special message for him. Walter wiped away a few tears during the reading. Each one expressed their gratefulness for the lessons they had learned because of the Mercantile. Beatrice caught Fredrick wiping a few away as well.

Beatrice did her best not to let Rudy take Ruth's attention, but she couldn't help it. Everywhere Ruth was, he was. He was doting on her as if she were queen.

The following day the Mercantile was a buzz of activity. The Mayor presented Uncle Walter a special plaque and said a lot of very nice things. Two men from the newspaper came; one took a picture of Walter standing on the front porch and the other wrote things down on a little tablet. There was a steady stream of guests who had made a special trip to help celebrate Reis's 50th Anniversary.

Sade had the responsibility for the food on that day. She had recruited Mother to assist, and Mother recruited Ruth and Beatrice. The four women spent the day in white aprons, taking direction from Sade and laughing their way through the day. Beatrice took it upon herself to keep an eye out for Rudy and every time he appeared, she would tell him that Ruth was in the middle of a cake, or mixing cookies, or assisting Sade and couldn't come out of the kitchen.

"He's like a bad cold," she told William, "I can't get rid of him."

That evening, as the last guest left the store and Uncle Walter locked the door, Mother, Father, Ruth, Beatrice, Sade, and Fredrick straightened, swept, washed dishes, talked and laughed until their sides hurt. When the final crumb had been swept up and the last dish put away, Fredrick called them all out to the counter. He arranged six goblets around a large bottle of Champaign, the real stuff.

"Ruth, would you do the honors?" he asked, and Aunt Ruth handed each one a glass. Fredrick took the wrapper off exposing the cork. He pointed the bottle toward the middle of the store, wrinkled up his face as his thumbs pushed against the cork and, POP!, the cork went flying, the Champaign bubbled out the top and everyone cheered.

Fredrick poured each person their portion and then he held up his glass, "To a man who has everything and has given everything to those around him, may we all follow your example." Fredrick raised his glass higher, "To Walter."

Five other glasses followed and everyone echoed, "To Walter."

"I am so honored to be here," Fredrick continued after everyone had taken a sip. "The Reis family has become my family and I love every opportunity I get to share time with you." He then turned to Ruth, "This woman saved my life, she has stayed by my side and been the best friend I could have ever asked for. And Beatrice, you are the daughter I would have wanted." Fredrick raised his glass again, "To the Reiss'," he said.

"To the Reiss'" they replied.

Chapter Twenty-Three

Fall had arrived and winter was just around the corner. Breckschnieder's was a bustle of activity. New decorations were arriving everyday and the prop room was overflowing with giant fairy tale characters. Hansel and Gretel were sitting in the back lot as room needed to be cleared for them. Beatrice had a front row seat to the deliveries; from her office window she looked directly down onto the loading docks.

Some day she would have an office with a window facing the street, some day she may even have a corner office, but today, she was enjoying watching candy canes taller than the delivery men, gum drops the size of a car, and crystal snowflakes measuring 10 feet in diameter, being unloaded from the trucks.

Breckschnieder's was once again having a good year; it seemed as if Fredrick instinctively knew how to navigate the empire he built. Beatrice watched him carefully, she had deducted that he was not a big risk taker. Fredrick knew his business and his customers. He played a very safe game. "Always protect the meat and potatoes," he would say, "If you're going to make changes, do it with the desserts." And that's just how he ran his empire. Beatrice figured that Ruth was his dessert changer.

Beatrice sat at her desk reconciling the previous day's receipts. She was interrupted by a knock at the door.

"Hey there, girl," Ruth said, as she stuck her head in the door. "Join us for lunch?"

"Sure, who's us?"

"Rudy Meyer surprised me this morning and we're having lunch upstairs."

"That's nice," she said, making her best attempt to be convincing. "This the first time he's been in the city since the party?"

"No, he's dropped in on me a few times. I would like for you to get to know him, glad you can join us."

Beatrice glanced down at the blank lines of her calendar, "Oh shoot," she said, "I've got a meeting this afternoon, need to help someone with training."

"Can't you move it around?" Ruth asked.

"I don't think so, not a lot of days left in the year, I'm sorry."

"Alright then, next time."

Aunt Ruth withdrew her head from the doorway and she was gone. Beatrice glanced down on the loading docks; Pinocchio and Geppetto were laying on their backs looking up into the sky. Beatrice grabbed her coat and flew down the back stairs to the café.

"Get your coat," she said as she passed Christina. "We have a lunch date."

"Uh...we do?"

"Yes, get your coat unless you absolutely can't leave," she paused, "Never mind, get your coat."

Beatrice was out the café door before Christina could get into the back room. She told her staff she would be back and she was out the door.

"Can I ask why we aren't eating upstairs?"

"He's here again!"

"Who, Aldo?"

Beatrice jerked her head, "No! Aldo, Baldo, he's the least of our worries."

"Your worries," Christina said. Beatrice gave her a look that sent a chill through her.

"Rudy, the creep has been calling on Ruth. He's no good. I know it! He has to go!"

Christina was walking at breakneck speed to keep up with Beatrice. "Where are we going?"

"The diner, it's got such god awful food, no one will see us there."

Three blocks away from Breckschnieder's, Beatrice opened the door for Christina. The two stood in the doorway searching for an empty table. The black and white checkered floor had a thin coat of grease; just enough to make you feel as if you were going to skate all the way to the table. The red vinyl seat cushions were reflected in the stainless steel trim. There were stools at the counter and booths along the window. Beatrice spotted an empty booth halfway down.

As the ladies took their seats, a waitress with the voice of thunder shouted out, "Be right with you."Beatrice waved in acknowledgement.

"So what's wrong with Rudy? He seems like a nice guy to me."

"You've met him? When?"

"He's met Ruth for coffee several times. They seem to get along. He seems really attentive."

"He's after something, I know it."

"After something? What, her money?"

"Maybe, I don't know. He makes my skin crawl."

"That's no reason to…"

"No! But it is a reason to be careful," Beatrice said.

"What can I get you?" the waitress said.

They ordered two hot dogs and a bowl of chili. As soon as the orders were given, the waitress turned and yelled to the kitchen, "Two Coney Islands and a bowl of red." Beatrice laughed. "Will that be all ladies?"

"Yes," Beatrice replied.

"It'll be right out." And she was gone.

"It's a world of their own, isn't it?" Beatrice said.

"What are you planning on doing?" Christina said.

"I don't know," Beatrice said.

"Please, don't do anything rash," Christina said.

"Rash? Do you think I act rash?" Christina just smiled. Beatrice took a deep breath, "I promise, I won't act rash, but it will be over my dead body that he will interrupt her life."

"Interrupt?" Christina said. "Maybe he will be an addition."

"No," Beatrice said. "I doubt that he has added to anyone's life."

"Here you go ladies, two dogs and a chili," the server said as she slid the plates on the table.

237

"Thanks," Beatrice said.

"Do you ever think about them?" Christina blurted out.

"Sometimes," Beatrice said. "I wonder who Micheal is screwing in Virgina and who Aldo is stalking in Italy."

Christina broke a smile, "So you think they made it alive?"

"Of course they are alive. Why would you think otherwise?"

"Well, there's the tape and the rope, not to mention the cement."

"Yes, they are alive and well and messing up other people's live – just not ours!" Beatrice said as she took a bite of her dog.

"All I ask is that you give it time. Talk to Ruth, talk to Mr. Breckschnieder. Just don't do anything quickly."

"Alright. But if he…"

"Don't do anything quickly! Do I have your word?"

Beatrice looked down at her plate and then out the window. The passers-by blended together in a blur. Faces of people she didn't know. Faces of people she didn't care to know. They were just faces, and wished the Rudy was one of them.

"You have my word," she said.

Chapter Twenty-Four

"This is going to be our best holiday yet," Beatrice said addressing a small group of sales people seated inside her office. "Mr. Breckschnieder has once again given the best product possible, now it's our job to sell it!" A crash down in the loading docks echoed though the office. "What in heaven's name?" Beatrice shouted.

A woman sitting closest to the window looked out. "It's here," she said.

"What's here?" Beatrice asked.

"They call it - The Crusher," she replied. Another crash shook the office and those in attendance were at the window gazing down on the docks.

"It's huge!"

"I don't remember how much it holds, but it's tons."

"Tons of trash."

"And everything is supposed to go in there?"

"That's what they say."

"Everything!"

"It bigger than I imagined."

"It would hold a week's worth of trash."

"More than that, I think."

The group watched as the largest tow truck they had ever seen, pulled away from a gray metal box the size of a train car. Six workers watched as a man in a blue uniform began to connect large cables to a box that had been installed on the far end.

"That is where the button must be."

"What button?"

"There is a large red button and when it's pushed, it crushes all the trash down to a fraction of it's size."

"That's nuts."

"We're the first to test it!"

"Really?"

"Breckschnieder's is the first."

"That's crazy."

"It's supposed to save 'trash space', whatever that means."

"Do you hear that?"

"What?"

"Look, they must have connected it. Look, you can see it from up here; that arm, it's like a big arm, it's pushing forward. That's what it does, just keeps pushing the trash forward into that compartment."

"Can you imagine getting caught..."

Those were the last words that Beatrice heard. As she looked down, she watched as the large arm pushed its way to the front. Then the arm pulled back and stopped. The man in blue pushed the button again and the giant arm began to move forward again.

"Alright, Ladies and Gentleman, I think we've seen enough for today." Beatrice herded the group toward the door. "I trust all this excitement hasn't allowed us to forget our purpose here. Our job is to sell as much as we possibly can and in turn we will create less trash to go in that...that thing."

As the last person left the room, Beatrice closed the door. She leaned back against it, holding tightly to the door knob. She walked back over to the window and gazed down. The small group of men were now standing at the door of the Crusher as the man in blue was pointing out the mechanics. Beatrice grabbed her coat and was standing on the docks among the men in less than a minute.

The door to the Crusher was waist high to a person of average height. Beatrice listened closely to the instructions.

"As you see, the door can be locked," the man in blue put a key into the lock and locked it. "I suggest that you keep it locked at all times except when it is being loaded. I also suggest that not everyone has access to the key." He turned the key and opened the door. "Once you have put all the trash in through this door, you'll close the door and lock it before you press the button." The man in blue demonstrated what he had just said. He looked around the group, spotting Beatrice he said, "Would you like to press the button?"

Beatrice nodded and walked to the front of the group. "It's this big red button. All you have to do is give it a push."

Beatrice made a fist and pressed it against the button. It was harder to press than she thought. With one final push, she heard the gears begin to grind. The chains rattled as the arm began to move. The Crusher moaned and groaned as the arm moved forward. It seemed to take a minute for the arm to reach the end and then begin to retrieve.

"And that's the Crusher," the man in blue instructed.

Beatrice stayed with the group until they disbursed, when she made her way back to the office. Taking her coat off, she tossed it on the chair in the corner. She moved to the window and looked down.

There was a knock at the door. "I'm taking you to dinner!" Ruth said as she opened it. "No excuses, no meetings! Just you and me. Be in the Train Car at 6:30 p.m." Ruth pulled the door shut and Beatrice looked down once again at the Crusher.

There was no way out of it, she couldn't come up with another excuse for not showing up. She only hoped that Rudy would not be joining them. That evening as she cautiously entered the dining room, she sighed as she spotted Ruth seated at the corner table.

"Joining us for dinner?" a voice said from behind. Beatrice grinned as Fredrick put his arm around her. "Ruth says you've been too busy for lunching. Glad you could put it aside for tonight."

Fredrick escorted Beatrice to the table. "My favorite people," Ruth said, as Beatrice sat down across from her and Fredrick took the chair next to her.

"It's been far too long," Ruth said looking at Beatrice, just like Mother did whenever she went home.

"I think it was Walt's party when we were together last," Fredrick offered.

"Exactly! Ruth said. "We even live in the same house, and I never see you."

"Can we blame it on the holiday?" Beatrice said.

"Ah, yes the holidays. Is it that time of the year again?" Ruth said.

For a moment, Beatrice forgot about Rudy Meyer and her fear of his attempts to steal her life. She forgot about the Crusher and the power she felt when she pushed that big red button. This is how life was meant to be. This is where Ruth, Fredrick and she belonged. She had to make them see it. But if she didn't, she had to make sure Rudy Meyer would not take it away from her.

"What is that enormous metal box by the docks? It looks like you've had a real train delivered," Ruth asked.

"The Crusher?" Beatrice replied.

"You know about The Crusher?" Fredrick asked.

"The Crusher?" Ruth said, "What the hell is a Crusher?"

"Not a crusher," Fredrick said, "The Crusher."

"The, a, it, don't care...what is it?" Ruth said.

"It's a personal garbage dump," Beatrice said. "They let me push the red button."

"No!" said Fredrick. "You've pushed the button?" Beatrice nodded. "They said I had to wait till Friday! This is not right." Beatrice and Ruth broke into laughter.

"My little Bea got to push the big red button before you," Ruth mocked. "What is the world coming to?"

The trio laughed and talked the rest of the evening. Beatrice took mental pictures throughout the night. This was the world she wanted to live in. These were the people she wanted to protect. This was worth guarding, no matter what the cost.

Chapter Twenty-Five

Thanksgiving Day had finally arrived. The dining rooms were set for the staff and reservations had been made for any Breckschnieder employee's family member who was planning on joining them for dinner. Beatrice's younger brother William had taken the train the day before. He spent the night with Ruth and Beatrice. He would work alongside Beatrice the next day as they set the window displays for Christmas.

Mr. Breckschnieder did his typical greeting of the guests and during dinner, made sure he personally greeted everyone at their tables. Ruth was late arriving and when she did, Rudy was by her side. Beatrice lost all concentration when they walked into the room. That evening as they were setting the windows, it was apparent that Beatrice Miller was in another world.

Christina had the café fully staffed and fully operational. It was the only time all year that anyone assisting is decorating could stop at the café for a break and Breckschnieder's would pick up the tab. William stood at the counter.

"I've not seen you around," Christina said.

"I'm William Miller," he said.

"Miller? Are you Bea's brother?"

"Yes, I am," he said.

Christina shot out her hand, "William Miller! It's so good to meet you. What are you having?"

"Beatrice said she needed something to get through the night and that you would know what she needs," he said. "Between you and me, I don't think she's feeling too well."

"Is there something wrong?"

"Can't say, just seems like something's bothering her," William said.

Christina glanced over at a window table where Rudy was sitting, William followed her glance.

"Has he been here long?" he asked.

"Since dinner ended," Christina said.

"Bea doesn't like him, I can tell."

"What can I get you?" Christina said in an attempt to change the focus.

"I don't know what I want, but you can give me whatever Bea usually has."

"How about this, you go back to Beatrice and keep an eye on her and I'll bring you your drinks and a little snack. I'll be there in about ten minutes."

"That would be great, if it's not too much trouble," William said.

"No problem at all. I'll be right behind you."

William returned to the windows and Christina prepared two hot cocoas with a sprinkle of spice and a stack of cookies all the while keeping one eye on Rudy. When Christina delivered the order, she couldn't help but see the despair on Beatrice's face. She set the tray down and grabbed Beatrice by the arm and lead her out of the window.

"Don't do anything rash," she said staring into her eyes. "Nothing!"

Beatrice was expressionless. Christina shook her arm. "Bea, tonight is about fairy tales and William, you have to snap out of this."

Beatrice took a deep breath. "Take another," Christina said. She began to see color return to Beatrice's face. "Tomorrow, you are going to make an appointment with Mr. Breckschnieder." Beatrice shook her head. "You are!" Christina said with unusual authority. "The two of you will figure this out. You need to take another breath."

Beatrice closed her eyes and forced herself to inhale. Life was returning to Beatrice and Christina could sense it.

William worked all night with Beatrice and at four o'clock in the morning, those who remained bundled up and journeyed outside to be the first to view the windows. As if she knew when the exact moment would be, Aunt Ruth joined Beatrice and William for the unveiling.

The three walked arm in arm from window to window, reading the selections from the original text and watching as the characters were put into motion. William had never seen such a thing and both Ruth and Beatrice enjoyed watching him as much as they did the display beyond the windows.

It took another couple hours before William and Beatrice got into a cab and headed to Ruth's. Once inside, Beatrice hugged William and thanked him for being with her and they both headed to bed. It was noon before either of them stirred.

Beatrice woke but stayed cuddled under the covers reliving the events of the night before. She was so glad she had been able to share it with William. Beatrice heard footsteps on the stairsembarrass. He must be up already, she thought as she forced herself out of bed. She slipped into a fluffy pair of slippers that Ruth had bought her, wrapped herself in the matching robe and headed down to the kitchen.

As she passed the guestroom door, it was closed. She continued down to the kitchen and to her surprise found it empty except for the large hairy creatures that bombarded her as she entered. "Good morning boys," she said. "How many are there of you today? Did Ruth add any new ones?" Beatrice made a cup of hot cocoa and sat by the window. The snow had begun to fall and she could only imagine the excitement that must be embracing the sightseers as they watched their favorite fairy tales come to life while big white snowflakes landed on their noses. She had to get down there to see it firsthand. It was the most exciting day of the year and she wasn't going to miss it.

As she headed back up the stairs, Fred snuck though the door and followed her up the stairs. "You're not supposed to be out here," she said, as she reached down and rubbed his head. Fred trotted up the stairs along of side her. Beatrice heard something drop. Fred heard it too and let out a growl. From the sound of it, it was coming from the fourth floor. She continued up. As she reached the third floor, she stopped to listen. Someone was up there. From Fred's expression, she was sure it wasn't Ruth.

"You wait here," she instructed Fred. "You're not supposed to be this far." Fred sat as if he understood every word. Beatrice began to climb the last flight of stairs when she saw a shadow against the wall.

"Hello," she said quietly, "Who's up here? Hello?"

"It's just me," a too familiar voice replied.

Beatrice made it to the top, "What are you doing up here?"

"Just looking around. This would be an extraordinary office," Rudy said.

"It is! It is as Uncle William left it."

"He had great taste, but it's a little out dated. And what a waste, this should be used, not kept as a shrine."

"It is how Ruth wants it to be," Beatrice said becoming more and more perturbed.

Rudy walked around the room and as he passed her, she wondered if she gave him a hard enough push would he land at the bottom of the stairs or get stuck halfway down? If he made it to the bottom, would he still be alive? Why don't they make stairs as one single flight? Why do these have to be landings? It would be difficult to get him to go down the entire way, but if she followed him, she could keep rolling him around the landing and down the next flight.

Jeannie Bruenning

"Beatrice, is that you?" William's voice startled her.

"I'm up here, just showing Rudy back down," she said. Beatrice stood at the top of the stairs glaring at Rudy. "It's time to go," she said quietly. Rudy took one last look around the library and headed down the stairs.

"One little push," Beatrice said under her breath. "One little push and it could be over."

"Bea, you coming?" William yelled from the landing.

Chapter Twenty-Six

Beatrice hailed a cab from outside's Ruth's front door. William needed to get to the train station to catch the train home and she was going to the store. Rudy had gathered his belongings and had left a few minutes earlier.

As the cab pulled in front of Breckschnieder's, Beatrice chuckled at the amount of people gazing into the windows.

"They've done it again!" the driver said.

"Looks like a success," Beatrice replied.

"You've seen them yet?" he asked.

"Yes, early this morning." She handed the driver the fee and opened her door. "I was in charge of setting them up." She exited the cab and slammed the door.

"Well, I'll be," he said and drove away.

Beatrice walked the outer parameter of the crowd and listened to the excitement. Snow was still falling and the day could not be more perfect. That is, expect for knowing Rudy and wanting to not know him. Beatrice entered through the café entrance.

"Good afternoon," Christina said.

"You're back already?" Beatrice said.

"I could ask you the same?"

"I couldn't wait to hear the reviews," Beatrice said.

"Are they in print already?"

"No, not those. The real reviews. Had to hear what the kids were saying," she said.

"And?"

"Yes, it's a success. How could it not be? When a giant so tall you can only see him from the waist down is standing in a shop window? It makes me feel like a miniature," Beatrice said. She took off her coat and sat at the counter. "He was at the house this morning?"

"He stayed overnight?" Christina asked.

"I don't know. I heard him up in William's study after I got up. Wanted to push him down the stairs."

"Nothing rash!" Christina reminded.

"Nothing rash," Bea said softly. "Don't think I actually agreed to that."

"You did," Christina said. Christina leaned over the counter, "Go across the street, take the elevator to the top floor and talk to him!"

"I can't do that! I've never been over there. I can't just barge in."

"This is your Ruth that you're talking about. It's his Ruth, too. Go talk to him!"

Beatrice sighed and rubbed her forehead.

"Go!"

Christina walked around the counter; she took Beatrice's arm and pulled her up off the stool. She walked her to the door and then out onto the sidewalk. "Either you can go on your own or I can walk over there with you."

Beatrice pushed her away, "I'll go on my own."

Christina watched as Beatrice crossed the traffic and entered the front door of the Breck Building. Beatrice walked to the counter to announce herself.

"I'm Beatrice Miller. I'm employed across the street. Is it possible to see Mr. Breckschnieder?"

The man behind the counter looked down at a large ledger that laid closed on he desk. He opened it and ran his finger down the columns. "Miss Beatrice Miller?" He turned the page, "Here you are. Of course." The man walked out from behind the desk, "Follow me," he said as he walked down a long hall.

"This used to be the way to the dining room," she said.

"You lived here?"

"Yes, seems like ages ago."

The man stopped at the set of elevator doors that once took her to the third floor. He put a large brass key into the lock and turned it making it light up. The doors opened, "This will take you to the eighth floor." Beatrice entered the elevator. The doors closed automatically and she watched as the dial above the door gracefully moved from floor to floor until finally pointing to the eight. A bell rang and the door opened to a beautifully decorated lobby. It had Ruth written all over it. "Can the woman do anything but perfection?" Beatrice said.

As she reached out to press the buzzer, the door opened and a tall, slender man wearing a three piece suite, wool coat, with a gray wool hat under his arm and a black leather briefcase in his hand excited.

"Good day," he said. "You can go right in."

"Thank you," Beatrice said, as she watched him pass the push the button to the elevator which opened immediately as if it were waiting for him. Beatrice watched as the doors closed and the mystery man was gone.

"Hello, who's there?" Fredrick called from inside. Beatrice hesitated.

"Hello?"

"It's only I, or me... it's Beatrice Miller."

"Is there any other Beatrice?" Fredrick Breckschnieder was standing in the doorway. "Miss Miller, what have I done to deserve this visit?"

"The man at the desk said I could come up."

"Of course you can come up, you are on the list."

"The list?"

"Oh yes, Miss Miller, you are on several lists. You are welcome anytime, come in. It's not much, but it's home."

Beatrice walked through the door into a very sparsely furnished apartment. The walls were beige and what furniture there was, was simple. She walked over to the windows and looked down. They were on the eighth floor, it was the highest she had ever been. The crowds of people below looked like miniatures. She was the giant looking down from the bean stock. She could see the roof top of Breckschnider's. As she looked out, she could see the roof tops of most of the buildings.

"Not a bad view," Fredrick said.

"Not a bad view at all," Beatrice said. They watched as the crowd moved around the window displays below.

"It's a good show, this year," Fredrick said. "You did an excellent job."

"Thanks," she said.

"But looking at the crowd below is not what brought you all the way up here," Fredrick sat in a modest leather chair and directed Beatrice to the other one that sat directly across from him. Beatrice removed her coat and sat down. "Tell me what's on your mind."

"I'm not sure how to say this or even if you are the right person to be saying it to," she swallowed hard enough that she was sure he heard it as well. "I'm very concerned about Ruth."

"Why?"

"It's not Ruth exactly, it's Mr. Meyer. I have a strange feeling about him and just before I left the house today, I found him in Uncle William's office."

"Was Ruth there with him?"

"No, he was up there all alone. He made some comment about how nice of an office it would make. I don't trust him. I just want him to go away."

Fredrick's expression softened and a gentle smile replaced his concerned look. "Doris used to say that. She had a sixth sense about her, she could tell within a few moments if someone was to be trusted. When they weren't, she would say they needed to be done away. I haven't thought about that for years. *Done away* and *letting go*, those were her two favorite descriptions. Strange thing, it was shortly after that they just seemed to do so. I always figured if she had the ability to stop them, she must also have the ability to let them go." Beatrice rubbed her hands together.

"The gentleman that was just here, you must have passed him." Beatrice nodded. "He's a private investigator."

"A what?"

"A private investigator, those are men who…"

"I know what they do, why was he here?"

"After our trip home, or your home, I hired him to do a little checking on our friend Mr. Meyer. He just left me the report."

"You hired someone to follow him?"

"They do more than that; they do a lot of research to find out history. Let me tell you, our Mr. Meyer has a little history."

"He's not my Mr. Meyer. I would like him to go away," Beatrice said very a matter of fact. Fredrick laughed.

"You sound just like her," he said. Fredrick picked up a file that lay on the table next to his chair. He slowly opened it, "Mr. Meyer seems to befriend women such as Ruth, marries them, skims off as much money as possible before they discover what has happened, and send him on his way. Interesting thing is, that no one seems to be able to prove he has ever divorced any of these women."

"Mother said he had women, I thought she just meant girlfriends."

"She may have. It looks like the marriages were all done secretly and quickly. Not sure why he feels the need to marry them, but he does."

"Selfish Bastard," Beatrice said.

"What did you say?" Fredrick asked.

"I'm sorry...I shouldn't have..." Fredrick waited for it. "Selfish Bastard!" Beatrice repeated.

Fredrick put his head back and bellowed. Beatrice couldn't help but at least break a smile. "My Doris used those exact words."

"So does Aunt Ruth," Beatrice said now laughing with him.

"They were the *bestest* of friends," he said. "I envy their relationship sometimes. It was as if they had secrets that they would take to the grave." Fredrick was suddenly somber. "She took them to the grave. There was always a part of her that I couldn't share. There were secrets in their relationship that were not mine to have."

"Why haven't you asked her?" Beatrice said.

"Asked who?"

"Why haven't you asked Ruth?"

"I'm not sure what you are implying," he said.

"She would tell you, she would tell you everything." Beatrice said suddenly feeling her eyes begin to burn as they welled up. "She loves you more than life itself."

The color in Fredrick's face vanished and he was now a lonely shade of beige. "She does?" he asked.

"You have everything. More than most men will ever have. You found the woman of your dreams and you lost her. But you have her *bestest* of friends who loves you beyond all your wealth, or success. Why haven't you asked her?"

Fredrick leaned forward and rested his elbows on his knees. The snow softly fell pass the windows and the sky seemed to have turned a few shades darker in preparation for night fall. Beatrice wiped a tear that had escaped her resistance. She watched the snowflakes gently float down out of sight. They sat in silence and the room became still and cold.

Chapter Twenty-Seven

Beatrice Miller sat at her desk and peered down at the docks. She watched as two men wheeled a large container out of the back entrance. They guided it over to the metal door. One man opened the door and the other dumped the contents of the large container into the bin. As one closed the door the other pushed the big red button and Beatrice heard the gears groan. As the bin filled, the nose of crushing debris echoed through the docks.

It's just loud enough to hide any screams, she thought.

It was a week before Christmas and the entire world was celebrating the season, the entire world except for her. Between keeping up with her responsibilities and keeping a watchful eye on *Rudy Tudy Meyer*, she was exhausted. Christina seemed never far away. Beatrice knew that she, herself, was being watched. In some ways she hated it, and in others, she loved it. Ruth had Doris, and Beatrice felt she had Christina.

The days grew longer the closer the calendar drew to December 25th. She hadn't seen Ruth in several days; they were like ships passing in the night. Her door was always closed when she arrived home and if it wasn't, Beatrice was fast asleep when Ruth came in. She hadn't run into Rudy, but she couldn't be sure that he wasn't always there.

Each morning, Beatrice would tip toe up to Uncle William's office to check on it. She was determined that if she found him there, she would roll him down the stairs and with any luck be able to roll him right out the door. Each morning was the same, nothing seemed to be moved, nothing bothered.

It was December 21st. Two and a half days of crazy business then there would be time to sit with Ruth. Maybe she could talk her into a trip to Paris, a trip without Rudy. Just she and Ruth, if she could somehow get Fredrick to go with them, she could at least pretend all was right with the world. Beatrice dressed, pinned on the gold pin she had worn every day since Uncle Walter had presented it to her. Pulled her hair up and allowed a few ringlets to cascade down the side of her face and slipped on the black leather boots that kept her feet warm and comfortable.

"Ruth hates you, you know," she said to each as she pulled them on. "Too bad we can't get Rudy to wear you, she may be willing to let him go."

Beatrice glided down the stairs and into the kitchen. She removed a piece of bread from the box and set it on a plate. As she walked over to the table, she saw a roll of large papers tucked in the corner.

"Blueprints! What is she changing now?" Beatrice retrieved the roll and spread it on the table. "The office? She wouldn't have the office... These aren't Ruth's - these are his. Holy Shit! He's already done it!"

Beatrice grabbed her coat and darted out the door. A taxi squealed as it came to a stop to avoid running her over. "What are you doing?" the driver yelled out of the window.

"I've got to let him go!" she yelled back. She ran around the taxi and jumped into the back seat. "Breckschnider's! Now!"

The tires squealed once again as the driver sped off. The ten minute trip seemed like hours. Beatrice had a five dollar bill crammed into her pocket; she pulled it out and threw it on the front seat as the cab came to a stop.

"Merry Christmas," the driver yelled out.

"Not yet!" she yelled back.

Beatrice bolted though the café door and breezed by Christina who immediately threw off her apron, made eye contact with one of her servers and stayed on Beatrice's heals all the way to her office.

Christina closed the door behind them. "Down there," Beatrice said pointing out of the window. "That's it. You don't have to help me, I can do this one. I just have to get him close enough."

"Stop!" Christina said. "Stop, right now! This is Ruth you are talking about. This is the *done away lady*, the 'oh deary, just let him go' one. She will know. She won't forgive you. This is Ruth Burrmann..."

"Did I hear my name?" Christina spun around and saw Ruth's head bursting though the door. Christina put her hand over her heart and signed.

"My, my, are we taking over the world?" she said. "Beatrice Miller, you have that look. Beige is not a good color for you."

Christina backed up until she felt confident that the chair would catch her and she fell back. "The tension is quite thick in here, ladies." Ruth sashayed over to the desk and pulled herself up, she sat on the corner and dangled her legs below. "So tell me, whatcha all talking about?"

Beatrice remained motionless as she starred out the window. "Quite a contraption, he has down there. He showed it to me last week. I couldn't help but think that if someone got too close to the edge, there could be an accident and no one would ever find out. Did you know they take that trash on a train to the coast and actually send it out to sea? Yep, send it sailing across the ocean."

Beatrice looked at her. "What are you doing here?" she asked.

"Haven't seen you for a bit, and I wanted to check up on you."

"You can go now. I'm fine, just busy. It is the holidays you know."

"Yes, the holidays. Parties, celebrations, my calendar has been quite full, but I always have time for my Bea." Ruth tilted her head and smiled at Beatrice. "Oh, that reminds me." Ruth patted her pocket, "I have something for you." She reached in and retrieved a white envelope the size of an invitation. "Here, this is for you. It's a celebration. Sort of a union or such." Ruth handed the envelope to Beatrice who took it and placed it back on the desk. "Aren't you going to open it? I think it has a deadline."

"I really don't have time right now."

"Make time," Ruth said stone faced. Christina looked up at Bea.

Beatrice took the envelope and opened it. It was a blue card with a gold outline of a dove. She forced her thumb in the crease and opened the card, it read: Please celebrate with us, today at twelve noon, the next line was Ruth's home address.

"What are we celebrating?" she asked.

"You'll see," Ruth said swinging her feet off the desk. "And you are welcome to join us, Christina. We would love for you to be there."

Ruth hopped off the desk and was out the door in a flash. A second later her head reappeared, "Twelve noon, don't be late!" and then she was gone.

The office was still and quiet. Laughter could be heard from the docks. It quieted and then they heard the unmistakable grinding of gears and meshing of trash.

"Meet me in the café at eleven thirty. Don't be late or I'll send the patrol out to find you." Beatrice starred down at the invite. "Beatrice Miller, did you hear me?"

Bea faintly nodded.

Christina left but every ounce of her wanted to stay. At eleven twenty-five, Christina took her apron off and replaced it with her coat. She took a seat at the counter. Eleven-thirty came and went. "Three more minutes, Bea, three more."

"I'm here," the message made Christina jump.

"Ready?" Christina asked.

"No, but let's go." The two women walked out the door.

It had warmed over the night and the winter snow had turned to winter rain, leaving the ground a sloppy mess. Christina put her fingers to her lips and whistled. Three cabs passed them before one pulled over and the two got in.

"Messy day out there," the driver said.

"Merry Christmas," Bea replied.

The cab pulled up to Ruth's address and sat behind another taxi. Ruth was standing at the door waving. As they exited the cab, they saw the silhouette of a middle aged man in the back seat. He was slightly slouched over with his hands between his legs. He didn't move. Christina tapped on the window, but he didn't acknowledge. For a brief second, Christina saw Aldo slouched on the floor just before Beatrice pushed him forward into the refrigerator. She shivered. The cab pulled off and the two stood transfixed.

"Was that..." Christina asked.

"It looked like him."

"Was he..."

Beatrice shrugged her shoulders.

"Come on up, ladies," Ruth called from the doorway. Beatrice and Christina slowly climbed the stairs. "Here, let me take your coats. What a mess out there. Rain for

Christmas, that wasn't on my list." Ruth took the coats and hung them on the coat tree.

"Was that...?"

"Who?" Ruth asked.

"Was that Rudy?" Beatrice asked.

"Of course," Ruth said.

"Was he...?"

"Leaving? Yes, it was time, time to let him go. Good riddens to bad rubbish, is what I say."

"But he looked..."

"Like he had gone away? Well, he was. Off to some exciting new adventure." Ruth walked through the kitchen door and motioned for them to follow.

"But Ruth..." Beatrice said as she entered the kitchen. She stopped suddenly. Standing next to Ruth was Fredrick holding a tray of china cups filled with steaming cocoa and a bottle of rum. Around them sat six very well behaved dogs.

"May I introduce Mr. and Mrs. Fredrick Breckschnieder."

"What?" screamed Christina.

"Mr. and Mrs.! You did it!" Beatrice yelled.

Fredrick put the tray on the counter and put his arm around Ruth. "Someone told me that she would do anything for me and she proved that today." Fredrick leaned over and kissed Ruth on the forehead. Beatrice couldn't hold back, she wrapped herself inside Ruth and Fredrick's embrace. Christina wiped the tears and breathed a sign of relief.

As Beatrice backed away, she saw the blue prints spread out on the table. "Are those yours?" she asked.

"Yes," Ruth said. "But before we do anything with them, I want to get your approval."

"You don't need my approval," she said.

"I want to make some changes to the library, Fredrick will need an office at home," Ruth said.

"You're moving here!" Beatrice asked. Fredrick nodded. "Two houses! You'll have two houses in the city!"

"Actually," Fredrick said as he reached into his pocket. "We will only need one. The other will be occupied by the new Director at Breckschnieder's," Fredrick placed a large brass key into Beatrice's hand. "Who just happens to be my niece." He wrapped his hands around hers. Her lip began to quiver. "We have lots to do," he said softly, "And a life time to do it."

Other titles by Jeannie G Bruenning

The Plan Series: *an allegorical telling of scripture*

> The Plan
>
> The Captive

Lessons Learned in Retail Management

> Vol. 1 While climbing the seemingly never ending ladder of success
>
> Vol. 2 The BEST advise ever

Children's Titles

> Mr Hobbins Beautiful Things
>
> Your Wagon is a Sagon?

Connect

www.jeanniegb.com

www.asilverthread.com